Literary Al——

by the
Ten Green Jotters

PublishNation
www.publishnation.co.uk

CONTENTS

Foreword

Suspicion   6
C. G. Harris

A (K)night to Remember   13
Tony Ormerod

Going back to Maple Lake   17
Janet Winson

CarDiver   20
Richie Stress

Can You Hear Me?   24
Dina Sullivan

Death Changes Everything   47
Richard Miller

Wasps   50
Glynne Covell

The (Other) Great Escape   53
Jan Brown

The Dawn Chorus   60
A.J.R. Kinchington

A 'Bunglar's' Tale   76
Julia Gale

A Post Mortem   81
Richie Stress

Starting all over Again (Part One): Soul Surfing   82
    Janet Winson

Starting all over Again (Part Two): Trawling the Catch   88
    Janet Winson

The Sloth   94
    Glynne Covell

Lighthouse Eddy   96
    C.G. Harris

Small Beginnings   104
    Tony Ormerod

Connection Lost   107
    Jan Brown

A Table for One   111
    Julia Gale

Squelchfoot   115
    Richie Stress

Taking a Bath   121
    Richard Miller

Needless Needles   124
    Richie Stress

Sleigh Bell Blues   125
    Tony Ormerod

Guiding Star   127
    A.J.R. Kinchington

A New Beginning 130
 Julia Gale

Mud Pie 135
 Richie Stress

Long Overdue 136
 Richard Miller

An Old Penny 140
 Glynne Covell

A Particular Man 144
 Jan Brown

A Point of View 146
 C.G. Harris

Hermes 148
 Richie Stress

Whatever Happened To…? 154
 Glynne Covell

Joe Renews an Old Acquaintance 156
 Tony Ormerod

Fatberg 162
 Jan Brown

The Visit 166
 Julia Gale

Statement 170
 Richie Stress

The Wrong Suitcase 171
 Tony Ormerod

The Winter Sea   173
Richard Miller

First Time Abroad   180
Glynne Covell

Pensive   182
Richie Stress

Looking for Maya   183
Jan Brown

About the authors   185

FOREWORD

This book is a collaboration born out of a love of writing and friendship, and a desire for the Ten Green Jotters of Sidcup to entertain the reader. It has been a challenging, yet joyous, experience for us to work together to bring these pages to you and our sincere wish is that you enjoy reading these tales as much as we have enjoyed creating them.

The writings of the Ten Green Jotters are of varying hues and we hope that you will find in this collection of short stories and poems a shade of writing to please you. If we succeed in this we will be Ten *happy* Green Jotters.

SUSPICION
By C.G. Harris

Let me ask you this – was there a time when you couldn't believe your eyes? I mean, you *literally* could not believe what you were seeing? If there was, did your jaw drop or did you just rub your eyes and swear to yourself? I'm telling you now I did all three when I saw a certain guy push his wife overboard.

It happened so quickly, and he was so *natural* about it – murder being such a quaint, inconsequential thing, of course – that I felt I just had to be mistaken, right? One casual glance round, one quick motion to grasp both ankles, and a swift heave, and she was gone. Then, a turn and stroll along the windswept deck and – get this – an audacious nod and smile to the steward as he passed him, and he was away. The trouble with something like that is it's so outrageous it just can't be true - can it?

I know that it *can* be true, and although I was drunk, I was feeling just sober enough not to want to get myself killed – so I stayed right where I was, hidden in the shadow of a hanging lifeboat, the large, motorised kind with plenty of room that they always use on cruise ships these days (lessons learned from the *Titanic*, right?). I didn't detach myself from the wall holding me up till the man was gone – and I mean *well* gone. Then, I stumbled to the stern and peered over the rails.

I could see nothing in the water but waves, churned to a white hue by the thrust of the engines. The waves settled and quickly merged into the blackness of the Pacific - it was difficult to see anything beyond them. Even the dim light from a crescent moon didn't help, given that it was partially hidden by long threads of cloud being shunted along in the sky by the south easterly wind. If there really had been a woman she was gone, left swiftly behind in a cold, vast and indifferent sea. It was a desolate way to go and I began to quickly sober up and ask myself what I could do, and what I should do.

Ok, firstly – had I actually seen what I thought I had? I shook my head to clear it and ran my fingers back through the hair I had left, then massaged my temples with both hands. I came to the conclusion that I had seen it indeed. I closed my eyes and tried hard to recollect something that had happened only a few seconds ago, but that already seemed like a distant dream.

The night was warm. Of course, it is cold in Alaska, but in August, with the ship two days out from Ketchikan on the return down to Seattle on the US mainland, the air temperature was a tourist-acceptable 66 °F. The woman had been wearing neither a jacket nor a coat, and I had recognised the same belted, light blue dress with white stripes on that she had been wearing when she boarded with her husband seven days before. Her striking yellow hair had set her apart, and I recalled thinking at that time how it seemed incongruous with her middle age. They had seemed happy enough, but I guess I was wrong – one of them had been very unhappy for sure.

Two other questions struck me. You may think it odd, but the first one – *how the hell is he going to get away with this?* – arose before the second, which should have been the most important – *can she be saved?* I guess it was less than a minute from the moment the woman disappeared until that question entered my head, and it suddenly made me turn and look for that steward, though I knew that the cold shock of the water followed by hypothermia was just as likely to kill her as drowning by the time help could get to her. I saw him on the upper deck smoking an illicit cigarette - the end glowed red and amber and a wisp of white smoke spun upwards and was shredded quickly by the wind. I was about to raise my arm and yell, when I realised I was not alone – there he stood, the *devoted husband,* silent and still, not five feet away. He was looking at me curiously, although in as unconcerned fashion as you like, and though my blood temperature seemed to drop a few degrees and my stomach muscles tightened, I immediately tried to adopt his casual manner, then, deciding it was best to take refuge in my drunkenness, slouched against the rails.

"Whoa, you seem the worse for wear." He said this in a cultured west coast voice with an amused look in his eyes that I didn't really like, but which I pretended not to notice.

"Seasickness," I answered, though the sea was only mildly choppy.

"Possibly a martini or two as well," he laughed. "Although my wife does suffer from seasickness."

"Is she sick now?" It was a foolhardy dig. I was befuddled and scared, but, irrational as it may seem, I suddenly felt annoyed at his nonchalance.

He shrugged his shoulders. They looked large in his tight, lightweight navy blazer. He looked kind of generally out of shape, even for a late middle-aged man, but I knew that he had strong arms – you can't throw someone overboard in a single heave without them, I know that much.

"She's lying down in our cabin right now."

There, I felt that doubt creep up again. He was as cool as could be – surely, I couldn't be mistaken? But when I closed my eyes, I recalled that tiny cry of surprise – not fear, but surprise – that had come from her trusting mouth and that had dissolved into the night as its owner spun and tumbled downwards. I decided I needed to get to my cabin, not only to straighten my thoughts, but because I was afraid he would realise that I wasn't as drunk as I was pretending to be. For me, that wouldn't prove to be a good thing for him to know.

I muttered a good night, and he raised a hand and nodded as I made my way along the deck towards the centre of the ship. I opened the door to the stairs leading to the cheaper cabins below-decks and chanced a glance back. I immediately wished that I hadn't; although the deck was not particularly well lit, I could see him leaning casually against the stern rails, with the now uncovered moon floating behind him. His eyes were hidden in the shadows, but I could tell that he was looking directly at me. He was rubbing his chin slowly, as if pondering over something – I could guess what it was.

*

Sleep did not come easily, or the morning quickly. Tomorrow, there would be one full day of cruising left. I had a feeling that it would be filled with self-doubt and indecision mixed with an awful lot of anxiety, and accompanied by fear. I lay on my berth throughout the night, looking out of a porthole through which I could see little but dismal clouds passing by. It was probably my imagination that heavy footsteps occasionally stopped outside my door.

The cabin was small, making me feel oppressed – the one my wife and I had shared a few years ago had been larger, almost grandiose, in comparison. It was not the same ship, of course; this one was of middling size, and revisiting our last trip together was a somewhat bitter, almost masochistic reminiscence for me, because she had left me shortly after. But I had certainly not expected to be lying where I was, thinking of another man's wife and the possibility that he had purposefully killed her. I finally slept.

*

I was once told that no matter how bad things looked during the day, they look a hell of a lot worse at night. The reverse must be true of the morning because when I woke and saw blue sky through that same porthole and heard passengers conversing, seemingly without a care, as they made their way to an early breakfast in one of the diners, my concerns yet again dwindled to a kind of nagging doubt. In all honesty, I had no idea what to do. In any event, although I wasn't sure that modern vessels still had them, I decided that I was not going to hide away below decks like a rat on a ship.

I risked a look in the mirror and saw what I had expected to see after the night I'd had – a slightly jowly face of fifty-two, eyes somewhat bloodied, with dark circles beneath them. I admitted to myself, though, that I was used to seeing my eyes that way – wine drunk to excess tended to have that effect. I reflected that it had been my wife who had often driven me to it. I began to feel a kinship with that guy if his wife was anything like mine.

I showered, then dressed in fresh but un-ironed cream linen slacks and a white shirt, and brushed my hair. I remembered how it had once been, longer and abundant. I was disappointed but resigned to the fact that was no longer the case. Getting older is a bummer for us all, but I wasn't looking too bad. I left the cabin and headed for breakfast, pretending that nothing was amiss. It was only when I thought of the guy looking at me the previous night that I felt the occasional prickle on my neck.

The woman first spoke to me at the buffet table. She was young - but not too young -of an age when it isn't totally out of the question that someone as good looking as her would want to strike up a conversation. It was, after all, a cruise ship with over 800 passengers on board; people do speak to other people... don't they?

The thing was, I didn't think anything of it, and we conversed over croissants and coffee. She was interesting enough – and interested in me enough – for me to allow myself to forget the previous night for a short while, and when she suggested meeting for a drink that evening, I accepted. We finished breakfast and walked out on deck, where I watched as she sashayed away, dark-haired and slim – someone, somewhere, was a lucky guy.

For the rest of the day, I alternated between curiosity and apprehension, sometimes on a crowded deck – I felt safer around people – and at other times in my locked cabin, sharing a bottle of cheap Chablis with myself. I saw no sign of the husband.

The next day, we were to dock in Seattle after a round trip – Juneau, Glacier Bay, Ketchikan and then home. I wanted…needed… to see what would happen when we disembarked. I felt that I couldn't be wrong about what I had seen – but many people, including the crew and the passengers, had seen and conversed with both him and his wife on the journey. He'd said she was in their cabin, but he had to leave the ship – how could he do that without his wife? I put off deciding what to do until the following day.

My head swam, only partly as a consequence of the wine, and it had not cleared entirely by the time of my date, but I made my way to the bar that looked out over a dark, balmy sea upon which the ship fairly glided, as if it couldn't wait to get home to port. The woman sat at a stool with a vodka martini, and although the bar was crowded, she had saved me a place. A glass of wine – full, but not for long – awaited me.

I guess flattery and attention after being deprived of a woman's company for long is enough to turn many a man's head – and I don't except mine. She was fun, she was pretty. There comes a time in an evening when confidences flow along with the alcohol, and a couple of times, I almost told her what I'd seen the previous night. I stopped myself, but only because I didn't want her to think I was mad or a drunk, and at least one of these was true. In any event, we made progress on other fronts. We exchanged cell phone numbers and addresses, and promised to look each other up. It was the usual vague thing that vacationers say and do - if I'd been hoping, in my middle-aged head, for something more tonight, it wasn't going to happen.

We went out on deck, and I said goodnight and watched her walking away – it was a pleasurable sight. She passed a man nearby who was leaning over the rails, looking out at the sea. I did the same. I think it was my imagination, but I thought that I could see the distant orange and yellow lights of mainland US winking at us in welcome, although I knew we were still many hours away.

I looked across at the man, and it was *him* – he looked back at me. He was dressed smartly but casually, and I put his age at close to mine; perhaps, we weren't really so different - apart from the odd case of homicide. We stared at each other for a moment or two, and I felt he still had this slightly undecided air about him. He slowly walked away. I shivered and retreated to my cabin.

*

I slept better than the night before, perhaps because I knew that things were coming to a head. When I woke and went upstairs, our ship had wended its way through Puget Sound, and we were coming into Elliot Bay. The Port of Seattle looked, as you might expect, full of bustle; the long winded aggravation of disembarkation loomed before us. My luggage had been colour coded, and I waited up on deck for my group to be called. During my wait, I scanned the gangway on the designated lower deck fervently for the husband; I was certain he would have had a suite, which takes priority over single cabins when leaving the ship.

Well, my jaw dropped open, and I swore yet again – the guy seemed to have a habit of making me do that - when I saw him and his wife, with a carry-on piece of luggage each, mingling with the crowds as they pushed and shoved along with the best of them. Her yellow hair blazed in the sunshine, and she was wearing that same light blue, belted dress, or something very like it. There seemed to be something of a kerfuffle, and her husband was arguing with one of the stewards, but she swiped her cruise card to debark. It was only when she was jostled and she dropped her bag and lifted her sunglasses, the better to pick it up, that I saw it was my pretty companion from the night before – my jaw dropped even further. She looked up, and that feeling you get when you know something is inevitable hit me. She put her glasses over her head with her right hand and looked directly at me for a

11

longish moment. Smiling, she pulled her glasses back down, nudging the man. He suddenly stopped arguing, and, with an angry gesture, he turned away from the steward, and the pair of them strode casually to the exit terminal. It was the last that I saw of them.

I certainly needed a drink. The interminable debarkation made me wait, which was just as well, because by the time I had claimed my baggage, I had decided to take a cab to *Bar Harbor*, a ten minute drive away, and finally think this one through.

I sat in the bar and ordered the most expensive bottle of Chablis that I could afford – a *Grand Cru Bougros* – filled a glass and raised it. Before I drank, I thought of my wife, whose behaviour had turned me into the drunk I was, and who had then left me because of it. I thought then of that guy who, for whatever reason, had taken his future into his own hands. All it had taken was a blonde wig, a blue dress, a lover to wear them, of course, and a diversion at debarkation while she swiped the wife's cruise card with her own.

I drank to him. I wouldn't be telling, and not just because, cold blooded as it was, I couldn't judge him awfully for doing what he had done. Nor because I had a suspicion, and my grudging respect, that he had committed the perfect homicide.

Why then? Because that guy sure knows how to plan a murder. And now he has my address.

This story was first published October 2017 in 'Light and Dark: 21 Short Stories' by C.G. Harris, which was shortlisted for the Georgina Hawtrey-Woore Award 2018 for Independent Authors. Book available on Amazon.

A [K]NIGHT TO REMEMBER
By Tony Ormerod

All was peaceful and quiet in the Nightingale sheltered accommodation unit on a miserably cold February afternoon back in 2010. Yet, in the comforting warmth of the communal lounge the residents, at least most of them, broke the silence by gathering noisily, as usual, for their mid afternoon tea and biscuits. Some then sat alone, lost in their own thoughts. One or two quickly fell asleep but in one corner of the tastefully furnished room three grey haired ladies, all in their eighties, sat around a table deep in conversation.

Edith, Flo and Maggie. The surviving three of the original intake in what was then a brand new building. The last of the 'Old Brigade' they told each other although other residents, perhaps a trifle jealous of their intimacy, had other names for them. 'Rat Pack' headed the list.

'Where's my teeth and where's that girl with my tea and Wagon Wheel?' enquired Flo.

'Look in your handbag Flo, where they usually are' said Edith 'and don't worry, I think I can hear the trolley now'

'Eh? Speak up, can't hear you.'

'Turn your thingee up' suggested Maggie loudly, patting her own ear by way of illustration, 'and look in your handbag!'

Flo rooted around in her bag then, triumphantly, pulled out a large handkerchief and magically transferred a set of dentures into her mouth in one swift movement, choosing to disregard the suggestion concerning her hearing aid. Privately, she resented Maggie's bossiness.

'Good afternoon ladies.' The trolley was wheeled into the room by Doreen, the Assistant Warden, who always made a point of serving the trio before everyone else. She was acutely aware of the pecking order in the establishment.

'What's good about it girl?' demanded Maggie sniffing. 'Take a look out of the window.'

Doreen, who was in her fifties, refused to be ruffled and, holding a large, heavy teapot in both hands over empty cups, she smiled and swung cheerfully into her routine.

'Who's for tea then my dears, and who wants biscuits?'

'Where's my Wagon Wheel?' an impatient Flo enquired. She had not heard a word of the conversation and, in any case, was not particularly interested.

'It's here love, as always.' Doreen raised her voice to reassure Flo and handed over the much - anticipated chocolate biscuit, in its familiar packaging.

'Not as big as they used to be are they?' Everyone, including Doreen, nodded in agreement. A 'hear, hear' came from a nearby table. It was Major Smith who, as always, was smartly dressed in a blue blazer, grey trousers, white shirt and his regimental tie. He was the only man in the place and relished the fact. Although he bored everyone with tales of derring-do in the Second World War he was tolerated. Doreen saw to the needs of Flo, Maggie and Edith before moving off to attend to others.

'Some folk', she thought, 'don't know when they're well off!'

Flo munched on her Wagon Wheel and, in spite of its diminished size, she was enjoying it. Something on the discarded wrapping caught her eye and caused her to pause. She spoke, loudly.

'I bet you two will never guess who I had a fling with once?' She looked at her friends and waited for some sort of reaction but there was none. However, Edith glanced over at Maggie and the look they exchanged spoke volumes. They were about to be regaled with one of Flo's stories which would no doubt be full of half-truths, or, at least, there would be some exaggeration. Distance in Flo's case not only lent enchantment but also prevented any attempt at verification of the actual facts.

'Well go on then' sighed Maggie eventually, 'is it someone we know or knew?'

Flo either ignored Maggie or did not hear her. She stared into the distance for a few seconds as if struggling to recall the details.

'Yes, I remember it now as if it was yesterday' she began. Edith suppressed a giggle.

'It was in 1944, or maybe 1945 when I met him. I was very young and like a lot more I had been evacuated out of London just before the start of the blitz in 1940. I finished up billeted with a very nice couple in the Welsh valleys and, after my parents were killed in an air raid, I stayed on. Nobody seemed to mind and there was nothing left for me in London.'

Flo paused and stared at the biscuit wrapping for a few seconds, as if for inspiration.

'Well go on Flo, get to the point' urged Edith.

'I'm getting there, I'm getting there. Well, although I was only eighteen I could easily pass for a bit older when I met a young lad, who was about twenty, at a local village dance. His name was Dick Jenkins; 'Big Dick' to his friends. No, don't laugh, we were all more innocent in those days.'

'Pull the other one Flo, nobody was *that* innocent back then.' Maggie was half-laughing, half-sneering.

'Speak for yourself Maggie and let me finish!' Maggie merely shrugged and shot a glance at Edith who looked equally unconvinced.

'Well, without going into details, he took me outside after we'd had a couple of drinks. I was not used to alcohol and, you know....'

'Say no more' said Edith, who was tiring of the conversation, 'he had his wicked way with you?'

'Well yes, I suppose he did, but I didn't mind. He had lovely eyes and a wonderful voice.'

'You mean he sang to you at the same time?' Maggie could not believe her ears.

'No! You silly woman, it was the way he spoke. Like music it was - well, you know the Welsh. I never met him again but I saw him a lot at the pictures, years later, after I moved back to London.'

'You mean you saw him in a cinema, with other women?'

'No, he was in the films, he was an actor.'

'Big Dick Jenkins? Never heard of him!' Maggie exploded with laughter, as did Edith. Even the Major, listening in attentively to their rather loud exchanges, joined in.

'No, don't be daft, that wasn't his stage name. I'll give you a clue.'

Flo picked up the wrapper and held it aloft. There was a moment or two of silence.

'Dick Wagon Wheel, what's he in, Westerns?' exclaimed Edith. Everyone laughed again. Flo ignored them and pointed to the maker's name. Maggie, who had left her spectacles in her room was nevertheless the first to react.

'What's that? Bartons? You met Dick Barton - Special Agent?'

'That's "Burtons" not "Bartons"' said Edith pointing. 'Dick Burton? Surely not, can't be, can it?'

'It can, and it was' said Flo smugly. 'I had a fling with Sir Richard Burton.'

'Not *the* Richard Burton surely?' Maggie asked hesitantly. She then added more confidently, 'anyway he was never a Sir.'

'Whether he was or not, I don't care, it happened, so there!'

'Fancy that' put in the Major from the next table. 'And he also manufactured biscuits!'

'Silly old sod' muttered Edith under her breath.

'Yes, I swear that every word is true.' Flo closed her eyes and smiled; she was eighteen again reliving the distant evening.

GOING BACK TO MAPLE LAKE
By Janet Winson

Lenny Maxwell could smell the newly cut lawns, all neatly matching and separated by brilliant white picket fences, regimental front paths led to the brightly coloured doors on the familiar sidewalk. This, the very neighbourhood where Lenny was born, the cherished first son of parents that had virtually given up hope of having a family. Here in this suburb of small downtown, Maple Lake in Vermont, where farmland surrounded the suburbs and the old railway station was just a mile or so away south of the small square church of St Crispin.

It was proving to be a bittersweet afternoon. Lenny was back here after five years of "being away" and growing up. He had wanted to come back to take a look again but being anxious, he kept to the shady side of the street like a thief. He just wanted a quiet time, reminiscing in this neighbourhood where he had known both the best and worst times of his short life. His mind free floated but then fixed strongly with memories of Junior High School. The swing park still stood, where Suzie Savini, shiny haired and dark eyed, had given him his very first proper kiss on an unforgettable but distant June afternoon. The swing park looked as it always had though that scrawny, freckled and carroty haired boy was now nearly six feet in height with a broad and athletic build which easily distracted the girls from his closely cropped, still flaming hair.

Lenny's life had gone terribly wrong in the summer of 1969. Everything shot to pieces in one crazy afternoon and he knew, without one vestige of doubt, it was all his own fault. The sap was rising and Lenny was popular with the girls and had been trying out every one of the forbidden fruits on his father's list, namely alcohol, tobacco and tentative sex. On a Thursday afternoon in late summer, just before school resumed and only a few days before his 15th birthday, Lenny drove off in his father's cream Pontiac convertible. The old man was out of town for a few days and the car keys had been winking at Lenny from the bowl on the dining room table, he only considered the consequences for a split second. He jumped into the driver's side, heading out of town towards Suzie's house. Suzie unexpectedly in charge of her little sister, Nancy, that afternoon, knew she would face punishment if her mother ever found out. She considered it was a risk worth taking and still exciting, even though Nancy would have to come too. The girls threw together a makeshift picnic, stolen from their mother's well stocked larder. Lenny sped off with the two girls towards Ferny Creek, a 30 minute drive in a fast car. He felt on top of the world.

Lenny was excited, loud and showing off. The powerful car radio was blaring out all the big hits of the season and the girls, sitting side by side in the back, were harmonising and jigging about in a world of their own. Unexpectedly and from nowhere, a mangy, yellow dog appeared ahead. The animal stopped, paralysed in fear and Lenny applied the whole lot of brakes nearly turning the car over. The girls were screaming hysterically in the back. Lenny could not even start to recognise his relief, when a huge truck behind, transporting animal feed, slammed into the back of the convertible. The truck driver cursed as he tried but failed to pull off the road. Time stopped for Lenny and the space before him. In retrospect he recognised the fact as if in capital letters with a double underlining of black ink. The Savini girls were on their way to the next world before the truck driver struggled out of his cab.

The scene in Lenny's memory receded from flashback initiating a severe cold sweat as he stopped in his tracks outside the old, familiar sweetshop, now with dusty windows and a rusty ice cream sign swinging outside. He could clearly remember squandering his weekly allowance here when he had to stand on tip-toe to see over the counter. He jumped nervously as he heard the shop-bell ringing followed by the door opening with a creak. Within seconds of recognising a familiar face, his shock developed into spontaneous adrenaline and Lenny took to his heels.

Standing in the shop doorway, Brad Savini gasped as he recognised Lenny's face, recognising the childish look of fear which was so greatly at odds with the powerful athletic shape of the young man. Getting his wits together, Brad began to chase Lenny. He had not seen him since the day at the courthouse when Lenny still looked like a geeky kid. Brad carried rather more weight than Lenny nowadays and soon struggled to keep him in sight. Brad still had his sisters' school photos on his bedside cabinet and lived a quiet life now with his broken parents who were unable to accept and let go of their girls, even after all these years. Life had changed drastically and tragically for all of them.

Lenny jumped the old, ramshackle picket fence of what looked like an empty house. The fence badly needed a lick of paint and repair. The whole place resembled a junk yard complete with rusty old mower and an upturned dustbin. Lenny knew Brad was slowing down and panting but still crouched as low as he could, trembling behind an ancient motorbike parked round the back. He waited a good while and when he finally got up, he kicked the empty beer cans lying on the sparse, weedy lawn with all his might. He felt sick, his heart pounding and contracting. He put both hands across his mouth to stifle his cries and rested his head against the wall.

Lenny would have to wait for ten minutes or so before he could safely make his way back to the railway station, this time going cross country. Time now to shut this door forever and continue the new life in Maine. Going back had been a childish fantasy and the worst idea ever. It had sickened him afresh. Some debts are too enormous to pay in a lifetime.

At last Lenny recognised that whatever life might tempt him with on his future path, these shadows would always be there just a few steps behind him.

CARDIVER
By Richie Stress

Ralph Tulley was fatigued. At first, his parents had been sympathetic, keeping him home and sending him for a blood test. Unfortunately, the results had been inconclusive and his parents explained away his concerns as growing pains.

'You must be looking forward to making some new friends?' said Ralph's mum.

'What?' Ralph did not bother to look up from his phone.

His mother cricked her head round from the front seat of the family Volvo. 'Are you looking forward to making friends at your new boarding school?'

'Oh, yes definitely,' he glanced up, forcing a smile.

Unable to shake off his exhaustion when attending Lexbey Grammar School for boys, Ralph would leave home every day, find a discrete hiding spot in some nearby woodland then doze until his alarm indicated home time. When he wasn't sleeping, he researched possible causes for his worsening condition.

The problem, he discovered, might be hormone related. Further intense investigation pointed towards faulty signalling between the hypothalamus, the pituitary gland, and the adrenal – the result being a severe endocrinal dysfunction. If left untreated, such a condition could lead to complete adrenal failure and even death.

Inevitably, Ralph's school dodging was discovered towards the end of the summer term. His parents had gone ballistic, accusing him of bringing shame upon the Tulley name and labelling his medical suppositions as melodramatic folly. He was excluded for the final few days of school and grounded for the entire summer holidays.

Unperturbed by this setback, and needing proof for his hypothesis, Ralph had borrowed his mother's credit card to pay for an online test. After spitting into some test tubes the samples were sent for analysis. Ralph prayed that when the results came through, they would prove his symptoms were real. Surely his parents would then see sense and help him before it was too late.

Two weeks later, an email arrived from the clinic confirming that Ralph did, indeed, have serious adrenal malfunction and recommending that he should seek medical advice. A cocktail of dread and elation fought for space in his throbbing, pubescent brain.

That very same day, his parents discovered the credit card use and decided, there and then, the best thing for everyone was to send Ralph away to school to keep him out of trouble. He had, of course, shown them the test results and tried desperately to explain the expected prognosis, but it was too late. His parents, believing none of it, had made up their mind and no self-indulgent, online spit-test diagnosis would change it.

Four weeks later Ralph shifted uncomfortably on the back seat, sporting his new school uniform.

'Let's put all this silly business behind us, eh son?' his father decreed from behind the wheel. 'Stealing your mother's credit card and bunking off school,' he said shaking his head. 'And no more of this quackery, do you hear me. Time to make a decent name for yourself now lad, hmmm?'

Fuck that! Ralph had every intention of making a name for himself, but not at some gulag education holding centre from the back of beyond.

Ralph Ulysses Tulley had decided to become a CarDiver®.

The so-called *sport* of car-diving had originated within the student communities of Japan, rapidly becoming a massive underground sensation, fuelled by a huge following on social media. Essentially, what you did – as a passenger – was to launch yourself from the back of a moving vehicle while streaming the event live from a hand-held mobile device.

Inevitably, there were casualties as competitors pushed for ever greater speeds. The trick, of course, was to go fast enough to achieve a record velocity, while avoiding the very real chance of death. It was ok if you sustained injury; in fact this simply added more kudos.

The rewards could be vast. Apart from the notoriety and respect from pretty much the entire social media community, a *CarDi* champion would have companies lining up to endorse their products; ever eager to cash in on the latest youth-craze gravy train.

'I hear they have their own tennis courts,' Ralph's mother declared excitedly.

Ralph logged onto Cardiver.com. After checking *yes* to the numerous disclaimers, absolving the site owners of any, and all, liability, he clicked through to the placings section. Number one was a guy called Lars from Finland. Lars had over two million followers and his own clothing range.

The only thing concerning Ralph, however, was the speed at which Lars' dive had been recorded – 51kph.

If he judged it just right, Ralph would sustain enough injuries to be hospitalised for several months, during which time he could get a clinical diagnosis and his parents would have no choice but to see his medical condition as a legitimate ongoing concern. Plus, of course, he would get all the trappings of being a *CarDi* hero.

Sweet!

He checked the speedometer – 76kph – way too fast. He needed, somehow, to get his father to move to the inside lane and slow down. He glanced out of the passenger side window. A scenery of green whizzed past at an alarming pace.

Shit!

He hadn't factored in the hard shoulder. How was he supposed to make a survivable landing onto unforgivable concrete? His stomach twisted in pain at this sudden, awful recognition. He forced a deep breath, trying desperately to consider his options. There were none. He prayed for a miracle.

Like manna from the heavens, a solution came. A sign; a literal sign in the distance, "No Hard Shoulder For 2km."

'Dad, could you slow down a bit, I feel sick.'

Ralph's dad glared at him in the rear view mirror, 'Let's not start any of this silly hormone business, shall we, eh?'

'Honestly Dad, I'm serious. I'm gonna puke!'

His mother tutted loudly, 'Well open a window or something; and don't say "puke," say "I feel sick."'

'Please just slow down a bit. Then I know I'll feel better.'

With a heavy sigh, Ralph's dad swerved over into the slow lane. Ralph discreetly unclicked his seat belt, holding it in place with his right hand and switched his phone to the video record setting.

He could see where the grass verge ended and merged back into the hard shoulder. His phone was flashing LIVE and there were already over two hundred thousand people following – most would be watching too.

The dashboard showed 60kph.

'It's helping, Dad. A bit slower and I'll be fine.'

300 metres...

His father eased his foot off the accelerator. Ralph leaned forward, surreptitiously panning his phone over his dad's left shoulder, focussing as best as he could on the decreasing speed dial.

54kph...

The screen on his phone indicated the reading as accepted and a fifteen second countdown appeared. He let the belt chord slide back into its seat.

'Look Ralph, a sign for your new school – only four kilometres to the next junction!' His mother clapped her hands together, in glee.

10 seconds...

Ralph moved his phone into his right hand, resting his left palm on the door release lever. He twisted his body to a forty-five degree angle, raising his left foot up onto the back seat as purchase.

His mother continued, '...the start of your new life.'

Ralph jumped.

CAN YOU HEAR ME?
By Dina Sullivan

James walked through the doors of Anderson, Smith and Butler Solicitors in Greenwich, just a ten-minute walk from his flat. After speaking to the receptionist to confirm his appointment he was shown into a small meeting room, where he waited. Presently a slight man in his mid-twenties, wearing a suit that looked one or two sizes too big for him, entered the room carrying a large brown envelope with *JAMES TREMAYNE* scrawled across it.

'Good morning sir. I have the package sent through from Porter and Dawes. I just need to verify your name and address please. Have you brought some I.D. with you?'

James offered up his passport and an electricity bill. The young man checked the details diligently, handed over the brown envelope and started to exit the room with the documents. 'I just need to take a copy of these, sir, for our records.'

Left alone in the dated, slightly dingy, but functional room, James tipped out the contents of the envelope. A bunch of keys clunked onto the table, followed by a smaller envelope, addressed to him, from Porter & Dawes. He ripped it open and speedily ran through the contents of the letter.

Moments later the young man reappeared with a photocopy of the identification documents and requested a signature to acknowledge receipt of the Porter & Dawes package. Having signed it, James thanked the young man, shook his hand, stuffed everything into the brown envelope and set off home to start packing.

*

Heading west out of London on the M25, he wondered what lay in store for him in Penzance. The motorway traffic was at its usual high-density level for a Friday afternoon and the July sun gradually began to cook him inside his tired, old Ford Fiesta. He desperately wanted to open the window but knew that his asthmatic lungs would not benefit from the 'fresh air', which was heavy with dust and exhaust fumes. He fiddled with the car fan to get some semblance of a breeze.

The seven-and-a-half-hour drive passed by uneventfully, filled with daydreams of his unseen inheritance and memories of his dad and Aunt Meg. The realisation that he was now all alone in the world, his aunt having been his last living blood relation, was not a good feeling. He shook his head and told himself to stop wallowing in self-pity. He had many friends in London, most of whom he knew through his work as a sound engineer, and he'd even brought some new sound equipment with him to test out while he was staying at the cottage, such was his love of his work. This trip would be part holiday, part sorting out the cottage and its contents and part work, although James never really thought of sound engineering as being work – it was his passion. July in Cornwall could be just what he needed.

A service station on the A30 was a life-saver. He pulled in and bought some basic provisions and an essential 6-pack of lager, then sat in his car and tucked into two rather dry ham and cheese rolls, a Mars Bar and a bitter cup of coffee, before setting off on the last leg of the journey.

The sun was sinking low on the horizon by the time he turned into Penhallion Drive. Passing a few isolated properties, he finally arrived at Stonecrop Cottage. The place felt quite remote, with only the distant, dim light from the last cottage he had passed giving any sign of life. He parked up on the gravel driveway and made his way, somewhat anxiously, to the weather beaten, wooden front door, showing its age with its peeling skin of pale blue paint. James drew a deep breath and exhaled slowly, puffing out his cheeks in the process. After a little wrestling, the rusty old door lock finally yielded.

The musty smell of the place was overwhelming. Instinctively, James reached for his blue inhaler and took a lug. The light switches inside the door were unresponsive. It hadn't occurred to him to bring a torch.

Idiot!

In the fast-failing light, he searched around for the fuse box, finding it under the stairs. Flicking those switches also failed to produce any effect.

'Okay – I need candles, matches.' He desperately scoured the room.

'Bingo!' He spotted two half-used wax ends on the mantelpiece alongside a box of extra-long matches. The soft flickering light cut swathes into the dark spaces as he held one of the candles aloft and glanced curiously around the room. The sofa and armchair were covered in sheets, which, when removed, revealed plain, dated, but otherwise well looked after furniture. A small kitchen was tucked away at the back of the property and appeared to have not been updated for several decades. Past the kitchen was one door leading to the garden and another to the bathroom and toilet.

'Marvellous!'

Drawing upon his short experience as a scout, James set about trying to get the log fire started to take away the dank feeling in the air. He went back outside to fetch his gear from the car, while the fire got going, and decided to leave the upstairs exploration until daylight.

Glancing round the room, first can of beer in hand, it looked as if there would be a considerable number of personal items to go through. *What a job!*

Rifling through a virtual stranger's personal belongings didn't seem right somehow, *but what else could be done?* James plonked down into the armchair and soon started to nod off by the fire. The long journey had finally caught up with him.

*

The crunching sound of gravel outside roused him. The fire still emitted a gentle crackle and a soft orange glow.

'Jesus! What the hell...?' James stumbled out of the chair as he caught sight of a hooded face peering at him through the front window. 'Who's there? What do you want?' he called out, trying hard to suppress the tremble in his voice.

There was a knock on the door. *Who on earth could it be? It's almost midnight.* He called out again. 'Who are you? What do you want?'

'Never mind who *I* am. Who are you? What are you doing in Meg's cottage? You'd better tell me quickly or I'm calling the police right now!' the voice of a young woman blasted back at him.

Whoever she is, she sounds like she means business.

'Alright, alright. Hold your horses. I'm Meg's nephew. I've inherited the cottage from her.'

There was a pause. 'Is that James?'

'Yeah, it is. Do I know you?'

'No - you don't know me, but Meg spoke of you many times. I'm Susan. I live next door – well, down the road next door. I saw the firelight coming through the windows and wondered what was going on. How about you open the door – or should we just talk through it?'

James opened the door and was pleasantly surprised to find that Susan was a petite, attractive, thirty-something woman, whose smile lit up her face as she stood in the shadows. 'Please, come in. It's nice to meet you, Susan.' He held out his hand and welcomed her inside.

'Could we have a light on, do you think?'

'I have tried but can't get the electrics to work. I guess it's been turned off since Aunt Meg...'

Without a word Susan went straight to one of the kitchen cupboards and switched the power on, instantly illuminating the room.

'Oh! I tried the fuse box under the stairs, with no luck. Thanks very much. Maybe you'd like a cup of tea now? Or a warm beer?'

'My pleasure, and a beer will be fine, thanks.' She gave a friendly smile and pulled back her hood, revealing a mess of short, red, wavy hair.

'I take it you knew Meg quite well then?' James asked, scanning her face as he passed her a can of beer. He found her pleasing to the eye.

'Yes, she was a good friend and neighbour. I was very fond of her. I noticed that you weren't at the funeral though. Why was that then?'

'Wow. You're very direct, aren't you?' James looked equally directly into her eyes. There was a familiarity about them that he couldn't quite put his finger on.

'Some might say 'feisty'.' Susan raised her eyebrows and smiled right back at him.

'Well, I only heard from the solicitors about two weeks ago. That was the first I knew about Aunt Meg passing away and my inheritance. We lost contact after my dad – her brother – passed away, about ten years ago, and I've moved home twice since then. I guess it took them a while to track me down. Thank you for going to the funeral, by the way. That was very kind of you. Were there many there? Did it go – well – okay?'

'About twenty people came along, I suppose. Just locals, you know; friends and acquaintances. It went as well as these things do. I've kept the cards from the floral tributes. I hope you don't mind that I did that? I thought you may turn up at some point, so I kept them for you. There was one that was quite puzzling actually. I'll bring them over tomorrow and you can see for yourself, if you'd like?'

'Yes, I would like. Thank you. I appreciate that.'

'Listen. I'd better get going now. It's late.' Susan passed the empty can to James, threw her hood up and headed for the door. 'See you tomorrow then?' she said with a brief backward glance.

'Looking forward to it. Night, Susan. And thanks again – for everything.' He closed the door and listened for the sound of crunchy footsteps as she walked back to the road but was surprised to hear nothing. Curling himself up on the sofa, he quickly drifted back into his slumber with the faintest trace of a smile on his lips.

*

James woke with a start, causing him to sit bolt upright, his senses shaken abruptly back into life. His pupils expanded as they struggled to focus on their surroundings. The fire had completely died out and the only illumination came by way of a few shafts of moonlight, finding their way into the cottage through gaps in the curtains. He guessed it must be the very early hours of the morning.

There it was again.

The sound.

It sounded like a girl or woman crying and appeared to be coming from somewhere inside the cottage. His senses guided his focus to the top of the stairs. The hairs stood up on the back of his neck as he froze to the spot, listening intently.

It definitely sounded like crying.

Or is it a fox outside?

He had often heard foxes at night in London. They sounded like a woman screaming or a baby crying. This didn't sound quite like that, *but still – it could be.* He tried to convince himself that it might be.

The crying – the sobbing – continued. The sound conveyed utter despair. It was heart-breaking.

What should I do?

James was too terrified to move.

Although he had never believed in ghosts, he didn't have the courage to venture upstairs and test that belief now. He decided that the safest course of action was to do nothing and just wait. Quickly and quietly he forced his size 11 feet into his trainers, purely as a precautionary measure.

Better safe than sorry!

After several more minutes the sobbing began to subside and gently fade away altogether. James sat there for at least a further five minutes, just listening – barely breathing. The only sound he could hear came from the fridge, which suddenly sprang to life with various whirring and clunking noises. Upstairs had fallen silent. He grabbed the door keys and car keys and one of the dust cover sheets, then hurriedly slipped outside to spend the rest of the night in the car, double-checking he had locked the car doors behind him.

*

The brilliance of the early morning sunshine, blasting through the windscreen, forced James to open his eyes. He was tired and hungry and aching from the discomfort of spending the night on the reclined front passenger seat of his car. Stepping out, he stretched his arms up and over his head, clasping his hands together for that extra stretch. For a moment he just stood looking at the cottage. All was quiet. The previous night's events, however, were still very much occupying his thoughts. It was time to be brave and venture back inside.

Steeling himself, he slowly made his way around the ground floor, bringing shafts of sunlight into the rooms by throwing open the dusty curtains in the lounge and kitchen. His eyes carefully scanned every nook and cranny, though he wasn't really sure what he was expecting to find, then he stopped for a minute or two in the bathroom for brief ablutions. He continued round until he found himself standing at the bottom of the stairs, where he stopped and looked up, listening intently. Hearing nothing, he started tentatively to climb the steps. There was a small window at the top of the stairs, dressed by a net curtain, allowing welcome sunshine to softly filter through. Everything seemed so much better – *safer* – in the daylight and James admonished himself for having been such a coward the night before.

The small upstairs landing had two doors leading from it, both of which were closed. He listened for a few moments at the first door and, once satisfied that all was quiet, entered. The room was full of oddments, furniture and memorabilia and had clearly not been used as a bedroom for some considerable time. The array of contents was neatly organised, as if ready for inspection. It would be a hugely daunting task to go through everything and an impossibility to get it done in just a couple of weeks. James' shoulders slumped, heavy with the weight of responsibility. Of course, this had been his dad, William's childhood home too, and the thought of finding some of his possessions here lifted his spirits somewhat. There was, thankfully, no sign of what could have caused the terrifying sounds from the previous night.

Stepping back across the landing he listened at the second door. Once again all was quiet, and he went inside. This was clearly Aunt Meg's bedroom. It was as if she had just popped out for a minute. Her dressing gown hung on the back of the door, her cardigan was draped over the chair and the pillow still bore the dent of Aunt Meg's head, from her last night's sleep. James shuddered. That was enough exploring for one day. He closed both doors behind him.

Back downstairs he made himself three rounds of toast and a mug of tea. He wondered what to do with his clothes. He didn't feel comfortable making space for them in Aunt Meg's wardrobe, nor sleeping in her bed. He didn't want to sleep upstairs at all for that matter; not until he had got to the bottom of the mysterious sounds anyway.

Maybe I should get rid of the bed, and other stuff, like clothing and bed linen. They won't hold any sentimental value. Then I can buy myself a new bed. Decision made. That would be his job for day one. First though, he needed to find a nearby shop to stock up on food and, more importantly, beer.

Before going out, he connected up his new recording apparatus on the coffee table and set it running, just in case there were any more voices in his absence. The expensive, high-tech and exceptionally sensitive equipment would pick up every sound from anywhere in the building.

He threw on some clean clothes and set off. Susan hadn't made clear when exactly she would be calling round today, and he wanted to try to be back in time for her arrival. As he walked to the car, he caught sight of the sea, which could now clearly be seen on the horizon. The sun was elevating quickly into the cloudless blue sky and the persistent sounds of squawking gulls battered his eardrums.

'What a wonderful place to live,' he mused. The salty sea breeze felt fresh and clean in his lungs and against his skin. It was a world away from London, where every inhalation was mired with choking pollutants. At least here he could drive with the car windows fully wound down *and* breathe freely at the same time.

Heaven.

It didn't take long to find a local minimart, where he splashed out on a trolley-load of provisions, before heading back to the cottage. Susan was sitting patiently on the doorstep when he got there.

'Oh, hi Susan. I hope you haven't been waiting long? I just needed a sustenance top-up.' He held up the bags as if to prove his point. 'What a fantastic place, isn't it? Well, I don't have to tell you, do I?' he rambled on as he opened the door and ushered Susan inside.

'I've only been here for five minutes, so don't worry yourself. I knew you couldn't have gone far. I've brought those floral tribute cards for you to read.'

'Perfect. I wanted to talk to you as well about something that happened here last night. I'll just get us a drink first.'

Looking intrigued, Susan sat down on one end of the sofa and tucked her feet up on one side, making herself at home. James made them both a cup of tea and joined her on the sofa. First, he switched off the recording equipment, then proceeded to describe the events of the previous night.

'Oh my God! How terrifying! No wonder you slept in the car,' Susan said. 'I would've done the same, I think. I don't recall Meg ever mentioning anything about strange sounds or ghosts. I take it you haven't heard anything else this morning?'

'No, I haven't, but while I was out I left my recording equipment running, just in case it picked up something else. That's my job. I'm a sound engineer. I just happened to bring this new gear with me to test out while I'm here. I've yet to play it back, but this thing can hear a pin drop at 50 paces, so if anything has gone on it will certainly have picked it up.'

Susan looked straight at him. 'Let's do it!'

He jumped up and connected the recording equipment to the amplifier and set it running. There was about an hour's worth of recording so, as the playback ran silently, the pair carried on chatting.

"How can you live with yourself? I hate you! I'll never forgive you for what you've done. You have blood on your hands! You may as well have killed her yourself."

James and Susan's jaws dropped as they heard a female voice coming from the speakers. The sound was a little crackly, but the voice was clear enough to be understood.

'Rewind that, James. Did I hear that right?' He effortlessly fiddled with the controls and played it back again. 'I did hear it right. *Blood on your hands*. That's what she said. Is she talking to a murderer or what?'

They continued the playback.

"I had no choice, Aggie. It's done." A man spoke this time.

They listened carefully to the remainder of the recording, but there was nothing more.

'Well, they were both Cornish accents, I can tell you that much.' Susan's voice cut through the silence.

'Who are they? What does it all mean? Where are the voices coming from?' He looked at Susan, his eyes pleading for some kind of help with it all.

'I don't think we have enough to go on yet, James, but you need to run this machine 24/7 until we do. Is that possible?'

'Yeah, I can do that. I'll also transfer anything we pick up onto a hard drive, so we have a permanent copy of it all.' He flopped back on the sofa in utter bewilderment. 'I just wasn't expecting this.'

'I think you're in a bit of shock. We need a beer. Re-set the machine and let's go sit in the garden. It was Meg's favourite place to sit, especially in weather like this.' Taking control of the situation, Susan grabbed two cans from the fridge and took them outside, picking up the envelope containing the floral tribute messages on the way. James was more than happy for her to take the lead and he dutifully followed her outside.

The garden was a sizeable plot. It had clearly been well designed and maintained, though it was showing signs of recent neglect. The grey-coloured and dusty shingle path wended its way through the flower beds and clusters of shrubs until it arrived at a small, long-ago-painted wooden bench, shaded by a beautiful, gnarly, old olive tree. To the right of the tree was a yellow rose bush, which someone had obviously tried to make a feature of by creating a surrounding pattern in the soil using broken pieces of terracotta pots and large pebbles. It was not an unattractive effort.

'What a lovely spot. I'm not surprised it was my aunt's favourite place.' James sat down, picked up the memorial cards and started reading.

The messages were all very kind and affectionately written. It made him smile to know that Meg was regarded so warmly by her friends and neighbours. However, when he came to the final card, he had to read it twice over to try and fathom what it meant.

My Darling Meggy
There has always been a space in my heart for the both of you.
If only they had just let us be.
Sleep well, my love. Until we meet again. Joe xxx

James looked up. 'Who on earth is Joe? And what does '*the both of you*' mean?' He sat and pondered for a few moments. His brow began to furrow in puzzlement.

'Maybe we need to track down this Joe?' Susan jumped in. 'Hey, I have an idea. I'll try asking Mrs Spencer. She was Meg's lifelong best friend. If anyone has any knowledge of Joe I think it would be her, though I can't promise that she'll be up to remembering. Sadly, she lives at Chyandour Nursing Home in Penzance now, suffering with early Alzheimer's disease. It's so sad. She was actually my headmistress at secondary school, so she should remember me, I hope.'

'I don't want to put you to any trouble, Susan. I'm just curious.'

'It's no trouble at all. I'll let you know how I get on.'

After Susan had left, James spent the rest of the day shopping online for a bed and bedding and making arrangements for someone to take away the old bed and the other unwanted items the following day. He heated up a ready meal, purporting to be a Sunday roast beef dinner, and sat down on the sofa to tuck in, staring at the recording equipment as he ate. It had been recording all day and, although no sounds had been heard from the garden, he decided to play it back anyway, in case something had been picked up.

After a long period of silence James took his dinner tray into the kitchen to clear up. A long, piercing scream exploded into his eardrums, followed by the clatter of his cutlery and tray hitting the tiled floor. The whites of his eyes grew in size as he strained to hear any further sounds.

What the hell was that?

The place fell silent again. Slowly and cautiously he crept back to the equipment, sat down and continued listening.

"What should we do with it?" A woman's voice this time.

"I know what to do. Give it me," a man replied.

"No! No...! No.......!" Then the scream came again. The sound of it seemed to fill the cottage and, just for a second, James thought he heard the sound of a baby, but it was so fleeting that he couldn't be sure. Maybe it was his imagination. He copied the conversation onto the hard drive, so that he could play it back to Susan, and set the recording to start afresh. Tomorrow he would start looking through Meg's personal belongings for clues as to what might have happened here. For tonight, though, he grabbed a few more cans of beer and headed out to the car. He wasn't yet ready to brave another night alone in the cottage.

*

The night passed uneventfully and James woke early, feeling dishevelled and tired. His confidence once again buoyed by the morning light, he made his way back indoors, where he washed, dressed and rustled up fried eggs on toast and a mug of tea. Then, with the aid of an old toolbox found under the stairs, he set about dismantling Aunt Meg's bed, having first black-bagged the bedding. The bed components and refuse sacks were taken out to the front garden to await collection that afternoon. The large mahogany wardrobe was a different matter entirely. Apart from the mass of clothes there was an assortment of boxes and bags to be gone through.

He started by taking each item from its hanger and checking that the pockets were empty, before throwing them into the refuse sacks. There really were a lot of clothes, some of which were clearly many years old. It was a saddening process to go through and he hoped that, if Aunt Meg was looking down on him, she would understand his need to do this and appreciate that it was being done with a heavy heart.

After filling five bags he moved on to the boxes. A large, brown storage box contained a pile of photo packets and several albums. They would take hours to go through, so were set aside for looking at another day. A small, decorative wooden box contained a few items of jewellery. Nothing of very high financial value, but clearly treasured and kept safely for, he assumed, special occasions. This was a keeper. Next, he came across a box of school books. James thumbed through a few of them, pausing when he discovered a book of poetry. The date on the cover was the year that he'd been born. There was only a dozen or so poems, but it was the final one that really caught his attention:

Three Goodbyes

Farewell to Joe, I wish you didn't have to go
My heart aches so, the pain will never go.

Goodbye little one, apple of my eye
Every time I think of you it makes me cry
No air, no voice, no life, no sight
Just disappearing silently into the night
I keep you as close as I can, you see
And remember you as I sit under the olive tree.

Au revoir little one, I was told to say goodbye
It's the hardest thing I've had to do in my life
I hope that one day you will know
The depths to which I love you so
Please forgive me, but the choice was not mine
I hope that all will become clear, in time.

Farewell

Goodbye
Au revoir

Meg

Wow! I think I'd better show this to Susan. James finished going through the bags and boxes, discarding anything that seemed unimportant and setting aside the rest for a closer look another day.

The caged, flat-back truck turned up to take away the first batch of clearance items. Then James settled down to play back the day's recording, even though he hadn't heard a sound. He was taken aback to hear the voices of two girls in conversation. He didn't understand how he hadn't heard them from upstairs.

"I don't know what to do, Jazz. I can't tell them. They'll go mad, I know they will. I'm scared, Jazz. What shall I do?"

"You've got to tell them, Mags. There's no choice. You've got to be brave. And have you told Joe? He needs to know. Your dad'll have his guts for garters when he finds out. You've got to warn Joe."

The conversation ended. Again, it was saved to the hard drive. There was so much to go through with Susan the next morning. He wanted to call her, but she'd said her phone was in for repair and she wouldn't be home until late. Somewhat despondently, he got on with making his dinner, re-read the poem several times over, and kept drinking beer until he finally stretched out on the sofa, in the safety and comfort of an alcoholic stupor. If there were any sounds that night, he didn't hear them.

*

The sun seemed to be having the morning off, being temporarily substituted by a blanket of low nimbostratus clouds coming in from the west. Rain looked imminent, but the knock on the door was enough to lift James' spirits. Susan energetically breezed in.

'I've got the surname!' she blurted out.

'What?'

'The *surname*. Joe's surname. It's Mackenzie. I visited Mrs Spencer last night and she told me that Joe had been Meg's boyfriend when they were at school. That means we can try tracking him down now. I'm betting that he's still in the area, or else how would he have known about Meg's passing?' She plonked herself down on the sofa, pleased as punch with her progress, and waited expectantly for praise to follow her revelations.

'Brilliant! Well done you! I'm glad that Mrs Spencer was able to recall that. How is she? It would be nice to meet her sometime. She may have more to tell us.'

'She seemed to be doing pretty well, but I guess that varies from day to day. Maybe I could ask if the two of us could visit her one afternoon? Don't expect too much though, will you? Aren't you excited about the news?'

'Yes, I am, but I also have some news for you.'

Susan looked at him quizzically.

'I have more ghost voices recorded. It's a short conversation between two girls. Also, I've found a great poem, by Meg, written when she was about 15. Here, take a look.' He passed the opened exercise book over.

While Susan read the poem, James set about playing back the recording from the hard drive. As the voices played Susan's mouth gaped open in astonishment. 'Oh my God, James.'

'What is it? What's wrong?'

'Well...You're not going to believe this, but they...they're not ghosts on that recording.' She stared at him strangely. Her breathing had audibly shortened.

'What are you talking about? Of course they're ghosts. What else could they be?'

'I don't know what they are, but I can tell you for sure that Jazz is definitely not a ghost.'

'And just how do you know that, Miss Clever Cloggs?'

Susan took a deep breath, struggling to utter the words. 'Because, James, unless I'm completely mistaken, Jazz is actually *Jasmine* Spencer, my old headmistress – Meg's best friend. I'd know that voice anywhere and, as you know, up until last night, she was very much alive.' The pair fell into a stunned silence.

'I'll, erm, put the kettle on,' James mumbled, as he sloped off to the kitchen, making himself busy while he tried to come up with a rational explanation for how the voice of Jazz had been captured on his machine. When he reappeared carrying two mugs of tea, Susan was still deep in thought. He broke the silence.

'Look. We may not know where these voices are coming from, but that's a separate issue that I'll have to try to work out by myself. After all, I am the sound man.' He tried to muster a smile. 'I really wanted your thoughts on the poem and what it could mean. We still have that and locating Joe Mackenzie to deal with.'

Susan shook her head, as if to clear it. 'You're right. It's just so bizarre though, isn't it? It's definitely Mrs Spencer and Meg. That's how Meg always referred to her, as Jazz. Okay, let me concentrate on this poem.' She picked up the exercise book again and tried to focus.

'The first verse seems clear enough. Joe has gone, for whatever reason, and she's broken hearted. It obviously wasn't their choice to break up. You can see that from his message on the flowers. The second verse is more worrying. The phrase 'little one, apple of my eye' could be used by a parent about their child. The word goodbye could be viewed as final. I think we can assume that if she had a child, then she was underage and Joe was the father. It's just not clear what happened to the child.'

A deep furrow had developed in James' brow. 'I've just remembered one of the earlier recordings. It said someone had blood on their hands. D'you remember? Maybe the baby was illegally aborted, or it died or – heaven forbid – someone killed it! We need to check local birth records for around that time.'

'I'm happy to check on that, James, and I'll see if I can find any trace of Joe Mackenzie while I'm at it. There's one thing niggling me though.'

'Only one?' James laughed.

'I hope I'm wrong, but Meg's poem talks about keeping something close by, when she sits under the olive tree.' There was a long pause. 'You don't think..........?'

'Strewth! I hope not, but it sounds like it might be a possibility. Maybe Meg has led us on this trail because she wants us to find her child? Maybe that's what she means by it 'all becoming clear in time'?'

'Okay. Well, I'll leave you to ponder on that, Sherlock. Meanwhile, I'll get on with tracking down Joe and I'll try to arrange a visit with

Jasmine Spencer for tomorrow afternoon. About three o'clock good for you?'

'Perfect. Shall I pick you up at two thirty?'

'I'm not sure what time I'll be ready, so I'll come to you.'

James spent the rest of the day looking through the photo albums he'd found in Aunt Meg's bedroom. He was starting to feel a little more comfortable in the cottage; a little more at home. And he was relieved to have discovered that the voices he'd heard so far were not necessarily ghosts, though he was no nearer knowing where they had come from. The childhood photographs of his dad and Meg really lifted his spirits and he took out a few special ones to have framed. He was enjoying thinking about his dad. He hadn't done that for a very long time.

*

'So, did you manage to find out anything about Joe after all?' he asked as they jumped into his car. *Damn. Why didn't I think to clean this up a bit!* He felt embarrassed by the food wrappings and empty beer cans strewn around the floor. It was not the impression that he wanted to create.

Too late now.

'Yes, I did. I found him in the census records, at an address in Mousehole, just along the coast road. I turned up there this morning, unannounced, and he was quite happy to talk to me. I explained about you and that you'd inherited the cottage and that we were just trying to find out more about Meg and wondered what he could tell me, us having seen the words on his floral tribute'

'And?' James prompted.

'He spoke quite freely, actually. He said that he and 'Meggy' had been an item for over a year, when she became 'in the family way'. They were both just 14 years old, at the time. They kept it from their parents for as long as they could, but when Meg's dad finally found out all hell was let loose. Joe said that her dad had beaten the living daylights out of him and told him never to see Meg again. He also threatened Joe's parents to keep quiet about it. Joe did manage to meet with Meg once more though, to say goodbye, but his family thought it best to move out of the village and that was the end of that.'

39

'What did he think had become of the baby?' James enquired.

'To be honest, he seemed a bit vague about that. He believed that the baby had died, he said, because he bumped into Meg about a year later and she had implied it.' Susan interrupted herself. 'Take the next left, James. The nursing home is about half a mile down on the right.'

James drove through the gates of the Chyandour Nursing Home and found a space to park. Inside they were shown to a comfortable seating area and were offered tea and biscuits, while they waited for Mrs Spencer. It wasn't exactly the Ritz, but the surroundings seemed pleasant enough.

'Hello again, Mrs Spencer.' Susan stood as the care assistant walked Jazz towards them. 'Can I introduce you to Meg's nephew, James? I'm sure she must have mentioned him to you many times.'

They all sat down and Jazz studied James carefully. 'Yes, I've seen photos of you. I know all about you, young man.'

James was surprised to be recognised. The woman before him appeared much younger than he had imagined, and it seemed unfair to him that someone so young could be afflicted with this dreaded illness. 'It's very nice to meet you, Mrs Spencer. Thank you for agreeing to see us. I just wanted to ask a few questions about my Aunt Meg, if that's okay?'

'Certainly, dear. What is it that you'd like to know?'

'Well, from what we've discovered Meg had a relationship with this fella Joe and it seems that she may have fallen pregnant. Do you know anything about that?'

'Yes, she did get pregnant by Joe. It was a dreadful time really. We were all so young. She was far too young to have children.'

'So what happened to the baby? We understand that it may have died.'

'Well, one of them died anyway.'

'What?' Susan spun round to face Jazz. 'What do you mean?'

'Twins. Mags had twins, dear. One of them was very, very poorly, but her dad wouldn't let them call a doctor out. It was the shame of it, you see. He wouldn't allow anyone to know. Poor Mags had to go through labour at the cottage with no pain relief or anything. Oh, it was a terrible night, she told me. Screamed the place down, she did. One of the babies died after about half an hour, and her dad buried it in the garden. It broke Mags and her mum's hearts. I don't think they ever forgave him. Mags' mum died within the year, you know. Her heart just gave up. It was the shock and upset of it all, Mags reckoned. She never forgave her father, not for the rest of his life. Wicked, wicked man!'

'That's an awful story. And what happened to the other child, Mrs Spencer? Do you know?'

'Other child?' Jazz's eyes glazed over and she drifted back into her own world. The visit was over.

*

After dropping Susan in town, James returned home, shocked by the afternoon's revelations. He still had much work to do at the cottage. He made himself a cup of coffee and went upstairs to continue going through the photos. He found a small album, right at the bottom of the box, labelled *James*. *Intriguing*, he thought. The album was entirely of him, from baby photos to every school year photo, through to university graduation. He'd had no idea that Dad had sent these to Aunt Meg, but then it wasn't really surprising, as she was also his godmother. The more he discovered about her, the more he regretted that he'd not kept in touch with her in his adulthood.

Suddenly his ears pricked up as he heard whispering. The sound seemed to be wrapping around him in the room. Terrified, he stood up and slowly backed up against the wall, as if to protect his back, fully expecting an apparition to appear. As his fingers spread out against the wall behind him, he felt the vibration of the voices.

The voices are coming from the walls!

He leapt away from it. The voices were too muffled to discern what was being said, but it sounded like children.

It could be a boy and a girl. Maybe Dad and Aunt Meg? Slowly, he moved back towards the wall and pressed his ear against it.

"Can I come to the beach with you, Will?"

"No, Maggie. Dad said you're too little. I'm going with my mates. Play with your doll."

He could hear them!

Wow! Their voices have somehow been absorbed into the fabric of the building. How fantastic is that!

He leaned harder into the wall, excited to hear more.

41

"Will. Get down here now or you'll get a good hiding, boy."

The voices stopped as suddenly as they'd started.

Stunned and shaken, James decided to take a break and sit outside for a while, at Aunt Meg's favourite spot, under the olive tree. The late afternoon sunshine had finally broken through and felt gloriously warm on his back. He soaked it up, closing his eyes and pondering on the voices in the walls. That's when he heard it. A baby's cry. It was so faint, he wondered if a family was passing by the cottage. He ran out to the front. There was no sign of anyone. He couldn't hear the cry either, so he went back to the garden bench.

Maybe it had been a gull that he heard?

It came again – the cry of a tiny baby. It seemed so near. And it was getting louder. He shivered, even though he was sitting in the warm July sun. The cry was calling to him, tormenting him. There was only one thing to do. He sprung up from the bench and headed for the shed to find a shovel. He had to find out.

After half an hour of gentle digging between the rose bush and the olive tree, the shovel met with something metallic. He dropped the shovel, crouched down and began moving the dirt aside with his hands. What had he hit? Gradually he uncovered the top of what appeared to be a tan leather holdall with brass hoops attached to the handles. He carried on digging until he had uncovered the entire top. Taking a very deep breath, James carefully undid the brass clasp, prised open the bag and leaned over to peer inside.

It was early evening by the time the local police arrived. James felt sure that, if she was home, Susan would have seen the two squad cars pull up outside and come straight round to find out what was going on, but there was no sign of her. He stood and watched as they painstakingly dug up the soil around the rose bush, under the bench and the surrounding area. It didn't take them long to extract the remains of a leather holdall from the ground. It was carefully placed into an evidence bag, sealed and removed to the boot of one of the cars. Nothing else was found. The officers were unable to speculate on the contents of the bag without further tests being undertaken by the coroner, but they confirmed that, as James had already seen, the bones appeared to be that of a very small baby. James willingly provided them with a DNA sample to help in establishing a family connection, as this was almost certainly his first cousin. The officer told him that he would fast track the DNA test and, with a bit of luck, the results would be available within 24 hours.

*

James spent a restless night on the sofa, listening out for any more sounds from the walls or bedrooms. He couldn't help wondering if this was the end of it, now that he had found the baby. He wondered if his dad had known about it. He would have been a young, newly married man, settled in London when this all happened, so may never have even known anything about it. *I suppose every family has its dark secrets.* The cottage creaked and gently groaned, but there were no more voices from the walls that night. Eventually he closed his eyes and fell asleep.

It felt like an interminably long wait before Susan arrived the next morning. James was more than pleased to see her. They sat down and he told her about the baby in the garden, the police and the voices in the walls. It was a lot for her to take in, but she did so in the calm, assured way that she seemed to deal with everything. Susan also had some startling news for him.

'I had an unexpected visitor late last night, James. Joe Mackenzie turned up at my door and asked me to give a message to you.' She proceeded to relay the conversation.

Tears welled up in James' eyes as Susan began to explain that Joe Mackenzie knew about the twins. 'He knew that the girl had died and knew that…'

'That what?'

'That the boy was given to Meg's brother and his wife, to bring up as their own. The other baby – it's you, James.'

Several minutes elapsed before he could speak.

'So, you're telling me that Aunt Meg was my real mum? And Joe is my father? Why on earth did they all keep this from me for all these years? And that poor little baby was my twin sister?'

Susan nodded and pulled James to his feet, wrapping her arms around him. He gratefully accepted this comforting blanket. This had been the most harrowing and unexpected week of his life. A new home, ghosts, a deceased sister, a dad he never knew about, the discovery that his aunt had actually been his mum and that the people

43

he'd thought of all his life as his mum and dad were nothing of the kind.

'Why didn't Joe come and talk to me himself?' James asked, pulling away from Susan slightly. 'Why did he come to you?'

'He said he was concerned that this news might be quite a shock for you, so he thought it'd be better coming from someone you know.'

'Well, he got that right. It's a hell of a shock, that's for sure. What a week! I don't think I could have coped with all of this without you, Susan. You've been an absolute rock – really you have.'

'No problem, James. I'm just glad I could help. But listen, I have to run a few important errands for my mum, so I have to scoot now. Will you be alright on your own?'

'I'll be fine. Don't worry. The police are coming by this afternoon, I hope, with the DNA results. Once that's all official I can go ahead and arrange a proper burial for my baby sister. I take it I can rely on you to come along to that?'

'Oh, I'll definitely be there. You can count on it.' Susan gave James a warm, lingering smile, kissed him affectionately on the cheek and set off for home. She always made him feel safe and comforted. That was the one great thing to come out of this week – her friendship.

Left alone, James started to think about his situation and the future. Pulling himself together, he scanned through the small ads in the Sunday paper for a local builder and circled a few names. He wanted a quote for removing all the plaster from the walls then re-plastering the entire cottage. He wondered if it might be the only way to remove the voices trapped within the building. He couldn't carry on staying there with voices from the past constantly coming back. It just wasn't feasible to live like that. As James was about to close the newspaper, his eye caught sight of a name in the obituaries column. Joseph James Mackenzie.

That can't be right?

He read it again. Joseph James Mackenzie of Mousehole, Cornwall, had died on 20th June – *two weeks before I arrived? How can that be possible? Susan only spoke to him last night.* He read on, aloud.

'The service will be held at Perranuthnoe Church at 11:00 a.m. on 10th July. That's tomorrow!' He ripped the section out of the paper and stuffed it into his pocket. He intended to be at that service and he needed to show this to Susan. *How can there possibly be two of them?*

A knock on the door interrupted his train of thought. It was Detective Constable John Hemsworth and PC Jones. They all took a seat in the living room.

DC Hemsworth handed James an envelope with the results of the DNA testing. 'It seems that your DNA was a match of over 99% with the bones found in the holdall, Mr. Tremayne. That would make you a very close relative of the deceased. We were also able to confirm that it was a girl and that she had probably died shortly after birth or was stillborn.'

James nodded his head. It completely tallied with what he had discovered so far.

'There was one other thing that we found, sir. It's a small silver pendant. It wasn't inside the holdall, but the examiner found it tucked into the outside pocket.'

'May I see it?' James asked.

'Yes, of course. Here you are. It's yours to keep, sir.'

James removed the delicate piece of jewellery from the clear plastic bag. As he examined it, the hairs on the back of his neck started to rise. The pendant was engraved on both sides. One side said James and the other side – Susan.

'Oh my God. I don't believe it.'

'What is it, sir? Is something wrong?'

'Nothing's wrong exactly, but I can't believe that my sister's name was Susan. It's the same name as my new friend in the next cottage. She's been helping me with everything.'

'What cottage would that be, Mr. Tremayne?' the PC enquired.

'The next one up the road. You can see it from my drive.'

'Not that cottage, sir, surely? You must mean somewhere else. That cottage has been derelict for a very long time. No one has lived there for about 25 years, as I recall.'

'Are you alright, Mr. Tremayne?' DC Hemsworth asked as he stood up. 'You're looking a bit confused, sir. Is there anything I can do to help?'

After a moment James gathered himself together. 'No, I don't need anything, thank you Detective. I'm not confused at all. In fact, everything has suddenly become entirely clear.'

'Glad to hear that, sir. Will you be staying in the area permanently now?'

James replied slowly and thoughtfully. 'No. No, I won't. I think that as soon as I've attended my father's and my sister's funerals I'll be putting this place up for sale. Sadly, there's nothing – and no one – to keep me here now.' James gave the officers a resigned smile as he showed them to the door, clutching the tiny silver pendant in his hand.

DEATH CHANGES EVERYTHING
By Richard Miller

It was early on 31 October 1517 and another typical autumn day in the German town of Wittenberg. A chill hung in the air and the sun was trying to peer through thick clouds. A few leaves still clung to trees but most formed brown and red carpets on the streets and in the fields. Market stalls were being opened; academics were heading to the local university; and priests and monks in the town's cathedral were readying themselves for another service.

Martin Luther, an ordained priest since 1507 and appointed as a Doctor of Theology five years later, sat in his room in the University of Wittenberg and stared at documents on the desk, wanting to send them to his overseer, the Bishop of Mainz, while also following the time-honoured tradition of pinning a copy to the front door of the cathedral. Torn between a rock and a hard place, he agonised over the right thing to do; commenting on theological practices and philosophies was not new but what was being advocated could antagonise the Catholic hierarchy. Having studied church history he was aware of the persecution that other complainants had suffered in the past.

A few days ago, Luther, being very angry about recent edicts from the church - especially those about paying for your soul to pass quickly through purgatory and being saved by good works rather than faith - had spoken to fellow priests. The troubled priest firmly believed in salvation by faith. Pondering the conversation, he recalled one of the debates with a colleague.

"Martin, you do realise by stating your wishes - or should that be demands - you could be opening up a can of worms and creating splits within the faith? You know your church history and what has happened before."

"I know, but I feel compelled by God to take a stance. If I don't, who will?"

"Yes, but it could lead to conflict. That's happened before. And what's all this about printing the bible in German. What's wrong with Latin?"

"But how many of our countrymen can understand that tongue? And shouldn't our people know that faith in the Almighty is all that is required for them to be saved? That's what was written down by our ancestors: even by Saint Paul."

"Be it on your head, friend. All I can repeat is what I've already said, in that what you propose could lead to disaster."

"I know, but what is more important: serving God or obeying the Church?"

Europe was changing. Explorers had discovered and created maps of new lands; the printing press was being used extensively to publish theological and non-theological ideas; and new scientific, artistic and political theories were being expounded almost by the day. Luther was fully aware that his views on religion could be seen as too radical and spark a fire which would spread and lead to major changes in society. There was also the fear of excommunication. Drenched in sweat even though it was a cold day, fear consumed his body and his hands shook.

Luther rose from his table and put on his thick coat to offer some protection against the autumn chill, but probably not against the cold blasts of anger that would flow from those at the top of the Catholic Church once his ideas had been studied.

Leaving the university, Luther decided he would first head to the cathedral to pin one copy of his thesis on the door and then venture inside to present another to the Bishop. The walk to the cathedral would be via the town market.

Entering the market, he noticed an argument between one of the stall holders and a few soldiers from the local garrison. As he passed the stall one of the soldiers struck its owner. Incensed by the action of the soldier, other merchants moved in to help their fellow trader. Even though it would delay him, Luther felt obliged to intervene and break up the fray. As he moved between the two groups of combatants exclaiming: "This is no way to behave!" a dagger pierced through the coat he was wearing and punctured his heart.

Shouts of "You've done it now, you've killed a priest!" and "Wait until the bishop hears about this," did not deter those involved in the melee.

As the murdered priest lay on the ground the documents he had been holding were kicked from his hand and trampled into the earth by those involved in the brawl. Luther's ideas would remain unread.

Historical Note:

Luther was not murdered and did send a copy of his ideas (there were 95 in total) to the Bishop of Mainz and they were pinned to the door of the cathedral.

His actions ignited the Protestant reformation in Europe and had a considerable impact not only on religion but also on science and politics. The break from Rome in England during the reign of Henry VIII is a very good example of the religious and political impact. Other reformers, e.g. Calvin, followed in Luther's footsteps. The invention of the printing press in the 15th century did help spread the new religious ideas but also new scientific and political philosophies.

In 1521 Luther was asked to renounce his ideas. By that time it was too late to stop the religious reforms.

If Luther had been killed, would others have proposed similar ideas? The 'ifs' and 'buts' of history.

WASPS
By Glynne Covell

Nine-thirty p.m.

Thwack! Thwack! Graham hit the wasps with his paper as they settled on the tablecloth.

'Blessed creatures', he groaned, 'What the hell is their purpose in life?'

It was unseasonably warm for late October, and the wasps were taking their time to leave the nest and die. The pest exterminator had advised him to leave the nest in place rather than spending money having it removed, being so near the end of the season. Graham, who was always loath to part with his cash unnecessarily, was more than pleased to hear that.

'A miser', his wife, Carol, had called him when she packed up and left a few months ago. 'A bombastic, aggressive, selfish miser!' He shook his head in disbelief, remembering her words but quite unable to understand how anyone could criticise him so. He would describe himself as a paragon of wisdom, caring, honest and modest; a man to be admired! True, he had risen to power in the company extraordinarily quickly, not because he had tripped colleagues up but because he had had the great misfortune to have worked with so many moronic employees who continually got in his way and just had to be eliminated.

Ten twenty-five p.m.

'Damn the blighters, they're in my bloody coffee', he growled. On the floor, he could see a dozen or so more wasps. Yes, they were slow, dozy and ready to die but while in the shower that morning, he found that they could still sting. He picked up the hand Dyson from the charger and sucked up the invading monsters. Quick, easy, final.

Ten forty-six p.m.

The television suddenly turned on, surprising Graham with extraordinarily loud music. 'Strange' he muttered, grabbing the remote to turn it off. *Technology* he pondered, *will control the human race one day.* He cast his mind back to the very odd experience some ten years ago when he and Carol had been watching a film on TV. Unexplained, terrific static interference appeared on the screen which, when it cleared, gave way to a blurry vision of two men in space suits who said very clearly:

'We are coming; we will be with you soon.'

More haphazard interference with buzzing and crackling followed before the film returned to the screen. It was a strange phenomenon and quite disturbing when Graham and Carol realised that no-one else had experienced it that evening. But THEY still had not arrived Graham thought, smiling to himself while grabbing the Dyson again to exterminate more wasps near the television plug.

Eleven five p.m.

Time for bed. Early start tomorrow. Need to get going on some more redundancies; save some more money. More cutbacks necessary rather than just relying on natural wastage. He swore, knocking another wasp from his face and pulled up the duvet over him. He cursed the Queen for making a nest in his loft! Damn cheek!

Eleven fifteen p.m.

Sleep...

Suddenly, startled, Graham opened his eyes wide in shock. An incredible, searing pain struck his hand and wrist. Momentarily stunned, he lifted his arm and then stared in utter disbelief when he saw that his whole arm was covered in a writhing mass of insects. It appeared to be twice the size and looked like a rolling, moving tide as it travelled further up his arm to his shoulder and neck. He leaned over to grab a pillow to swat them, but as he did so, another swarm landed on his face. Burning hot stings continuously attacked his cheek, again and again. Such excruciating pain he had never experienced before. The noise from the thousands of marauding wasps was intolerable. Deafening. Sickening. He screamed and screamed in terror. 'This can't be true! This cannot be happening!' But no, it was! This was real, and now he could feel the impossible, horrific sensation of the creatures entering his nostrils, his ears and mouth. He struggled to breathe.

51

'Dear God, save me', he whimpered.

Looking on, before they covered his eyes, the wasps now appeared to transform into tiny spacemen with yellow and black suits, multiplying into a hideous mass taking over the moving bed. His very last sight was of one staring at him, looking mean, threatening and demonic…

THEY had arrived.

THE (OTHER) GREAT ESCAPE

By Jan Brown

It seemed to Robert that death always came on a Sunday afternoon. Felt like death anyway. You've had your lunch, now have a little rest before tea. Or the phrase favoured by the new guard, get some shut-eye. Huh, shut your own eyes if you're that keen.

The objective was the nearest fire exit. Robert wheeled himself cautiously across the now deserted dining room, wrinkling his nose at the enduring mingling odours of cabbage and boiled bacon. As he negotiated his passage around clusters of padded dining chairs one of Robert's wheels began to squeak and he cursed to himself, another trap set by the enemy.

I don't need the wheelchair, he had insisted during the induction day tour.

However, it had proved difficult to resist, an easy option when his body was tired.

'Mr Alton, what are you doing?'

Robert looked up slowly, using the time to think.

'I, ah... I lost my way to my room.'

'Luckily I can help you with that sir. Come along, time for you to have a rest.'

Robert nodded wordlessly as the care worker pushed his wheelchair across the dining room. A potential advance foiled by a bloody squeaky wheel.

A full five minutes after being settled onto his bed by the care worker Robert paced his room, slowly of course, but he could do that. Stop relying on the dammed wheelchair, he told himself. Nothing wrong with his hearing though as he perceived the gentlest of taps on the door.

'Bob, Bob, are you there?'

'How many times do I have to tell you man, my name is Robert.'

'Ay, you can tell me all you like. I'll not waste two syllables on an Englishman when one will do. Let me in quick before someone hears us.'

Donald Argyle, having shut the door behind him, grabbed Robert's hand and pumped it up and down enthusiastically.

'Well done, Bob. I heard about your escape attempt, brave, although some might say foolhardy.'

He clutched his chest and sat down abruptly on the end of Robert's neatly made bed.

'Are you alright?' Robert asked brusquely.

'I'm fine, Bob. I just got myself a little over-excited with following your shenanigans. Do you have any of the hard stuff hidden away in this cell?'

'How many times do I have to remind you, it's Robert.'

'Ay, thanks, Bob.'

Donald took the beaker, plastic of course, but the golden liquid sparkled just as beautifully as if encased in finest crystal.

'Cheers, Bob.' He raised his beaker. 'You know you can call me Donnie.'

Three hours later the alarm sounded for tea, the jangling urgency making them clutch each other, how funny!

'A bit like the air raid siren d'you think?'

'Huh!' Robert frowned. 'More like the announcement of the Commandant's arrival.'

'Hmm, she does have a certain air about her,' Donnie concurred.

Giggling together they made their way carefully towards the dining room, Robert having wisely hidden the empty whisky bottle in an old wellington boot kept especially for such occasions.

'Eyes aware, she's on the door.' Robert nudged his companion.

'That I can see with my own eyes,' Donnie retorted. 'Just follow my lead.'

'Mr Alton, Mr Argyle?!' Mrs Pettifont, tall and angular, looked down at them. 'Gentlemen, good of you to join us.' She leaned forward almost as if to embrace the pair and recoiled, twitching her nose. 'I believe you may have broken a house rule… again.'

Donnie, fascinated by the speed and manoeuvrability of her extensive eyebrows, was for once lost for words.

'Err, which one?' Robert was aware of stifled sniggering from the occupants of the nearest table.

Mrs Pettifont screwed up her face with annoyance. 'Yes, that is exactly my point with you two. You don't even know which rule you're breaking. Well, you are living on borrowed time here as far as I'm concerned, I'm writing to your families.' She did her twitchy, flouncy thing and was gone.

'How does she do that?' Donnie muttered. 'She's no' a real person, disappearing like that, and the eyebrows, you have to admit they're magnificent.'

Having made their way to a vacant table Robert shook his head sorrowfully at Donnie. 'You completely lost your nerve back there and made me look an absolute fool.'

Donnie smirked. 'And your point is?'

Choosing to ignore his companion Robert looked cautiously around the dining room. There were still too many clusters of twittering ladies of a certain age for his liking, waiting to pounce. They couldn't seem to understand that he didn't want to meet a lady companion or go to the tea dances; he had loved his Margaret and now she was gone. To top it all his son had seen fit to entomb him in a residential home for the elderly, and he didn't feel elderly.

'Hi, you two. If you're quick I can still get you some tea.' Neither had noticed Amy's arrival but both appreciated this kindness from the young care assistant.

'Lashings of hot tea and buttered crumpets please, young Amy.' Robert twinkled winningly at her. She had more than a passing resemblance to his oldest granddaughter, or so he thought; he hadn't seen her for a while.

She grinned at them both. 'I think it's more a case of whatever's left. It's been really busy this evening and you were a bit late.' Amy set down a blue-and-white striped teapot and matching mugs before heading off to the kitchen.

Robert and Donnie sat silently, surrounded by the gentle subdued murmurings from neighbouring tables. Robert stared gloomily at the steam swirling from the spout. 'Why do we have to have mugs? Margaret and I always had proper cups and saucers.'

'The ladies always like a cup,' Donnie responded, 'but mugs suit us because we're a pair of mugs to have got stuck in this place!' He nudged Robert, apparently delighted at his joke. 'So what's the plan, Bob? How are we going to get out of here?'

'I don't think that we have anywhere to go to anyway.' Robert felt suddenly weary, even the effort of correcting Donnie about his name felt too much.

'Oh, come on, where's that famous Dunkirk spirit?' Donnie leaned in. 'Not a bit chicken are you?'

'I wasn't quite old enough for Dunkirk,' Robert snapped, 'though no doubt you were there.'

'Look, Bob, I don't want anyone else to hear this.' Donnie gestured for him to come closer.

'You know what they say about the walls having ears. I have an idea, something I've wanted to do for a long time now.' Donnie pulled the plate of tuna sandwiches, which Amy had placed on the table, towards him and began to devour one, much to Robert's annoyance.

'Do you make a habit of eating other residents' food?' he enquired in a prickly tone, bringing a sheepish grin from Donnie.

'Well, no, but I didn't think you'd mind as I've already drunk your whisky and I'm about to share my amazing idea.'

Robert eyed him doubtfully but nodded. 'Well, get on with it man.'

'I want to go to a rock concert,' Donnie announced. In the stunned silence he continued quickly. 'And I hoped that you, as the only other reasonably alive person in this place, would be interested in coming with me.'

Robert stared as a trolley stacked with half-eaten buns and curling sandwiches interspersed with teapots and mugs, some imprinted with lipstick, was wheeled past. 'Who were you planning on seeing?' he heard himself ask, amazed at his ability to sound quite normal. In fact, they sounded as though they were discussing where to go for a pub lunch.

'Black Sabbath tribute band,' said Donnie, sticking out his lower lip and nodding vigorously at his companion.

Robert stared at him with growing horror. *He's seriously considering this?* Feeling as if he were being sucked backwards at great speed down a big hole he struggled unsteadily to his feet, holding onto the table for support. 'Are you mad? Why in God's name would you want to go rushing off to see some second-rate has-beens? Black Death did you say?'

Donnie chuckled and reached for another sandwich. 'I like it, great name but no, not quite, it's Black Sabbath. So what do you think? Are you game?'

'Can I ask why you want to do this Donald?' Robert enquired. 'Are you a particular fan?'

'No, I've never seen them. I've read about them and heard them on my grandson's thing, some gadget that plays music.' Donnie smiled, reliving a happy memory.

'And you thought they were great musicians along the lines of Beethoven or Mozart?' Robert persisted sarcastically.

'God, no, I thought they were terrible, awful noise.' He registered that Robert was hovering there, still leaning unsteadily over the table, not wanting to be involved but at the same time perversely fascinated. His crumpled face creased even further with confusion.

Robert asked, 'Why do you want to go and see them then if they're not even the real thing?'

'Because I can, because we can.' Donnie rubbed his hands together enthusiastically. 'Look around you, they're bored and boring, you're bored and fed up. Let's go and have at least one adventure before we're incapable of even going to the toilet by ourselves.'

Donnie's impassioned speech, which had been heard by most of the other residents remaining in the dining room, had left him with a very red face. 'So will you come with me?' Donnie asked, sounding like a small child.

Robert, who had by now slumped back onto his chair, was curiously reminded of the popular 1950s painting – The Crying Boy. He and Margaret had been proud to hang a version of it over the fireplace in their first home. He smiled to himself now, thinking how they had happily left it there 25 years later when moving out and moving on.

Looking at Donnie, Robert shook his head. 'I cannot believe I'm saying this to you, you of all people in here can be insufferable, but yes, God help me, I'll come with you.'

*

They left Sunset Lodge the next morning, ironically well before sunrise, with the fresh dew glittering on the grass tips, the only witness to their departure a plump black-and-white cat. He had observed them with apparent indifference before resuming his careful washing regime.

Donnie had insisted on taking the motorised wheelchair. 'We won't get very far,' he had pointed out matter-of-factly, 'if you can't take two steps without having a rest!'

'You exaggerate as usual,' Robert had muttered but the wheelchair was taken, its use secured by a generous liquid donation to one of the more liberal members of staff.

Bus journey completed, tickets purchased and correct destination confirmed they sat on platform 4 of Orpington station, waiting for the Hastings train. They had agreed it would be best to wait for the off-peak service, but Donnie now tutted with annoyance as the departure board clicked on. 'Four minutes late now.'

'It feels like we're normal people sitting here.' Robert nodded genially at the small collection of travellers; at 9.42 it was just the very last stragglers of the rush hour crowd, and a relaxed air hung over the station.

'What d'you mean? We are normal.' Donnie continued to stare at the departure board, his mouth set in a tense line. 'We've not got two heads or anything.'

Robert chuckled. 'You know what I mean. Once you're old you suddenly become different, or at least people think you're different or they don't even notice you at all. He raised his Styrofoam tea container and touched it to Donnie's. 'But I have to admit you were right, this is fun. In fact, I might do it again.'

'Damn, I knew it!' Donnie exploded, pointing up at the departure board. 'Hastings train cancelled, bloody incompetent idiots couldn't run a hot water tap.'

Robert looked at him with concern. 'It's not the end of the world, is it? We'll just wait for the next one.'

'I just wanted it to be perfect,' Donnie appeared on the verge of tears, 'just this once.'

'Why is this trip really so important to you, Donnie?' Robert asked quietly.

Conversation was abruptly suspended as a fast London-bound express train chose that moment to hurtle through the station, whipping up discarded crisp packets and papers before rushing off down the tracks and disappearing, the platform and its inhabitants held momentarily in the ensuing hushed bubble of silence.

Donnie suddenly broke the spell. 'If you must know, my ex-wife was a big fan of the band, the real lot not these imposters, back in the 70s.'

'I didn't even know you were married!' Robert exclaimed.

'She left me for an orthodontist.' Donnie picked off bits of Styrofoam and rolled them between finger and thumb. 'She always had a thing about teeth.'

'So you still love her?' Robert hazarded a guess.

'We parted on awful terms. I told her to get out of my life forever.'

'Well, that's fair enough surely if she was making you that unhappy.'

'But I didn't mean it,' Donnie wailed suddenly. 'We never spoke again and she died in a stupid car crash.' He crushed the remains of the Styrofoam cup, the cooling tea finding an escape route as it bubbled out over his hands.

The silence threatened to stretch out, Donnie's admission hanging like a chasm between them, and Robert patted him awkwardly on the shoulder. 'I'm sorry, Donnie, I don't know what to say.' Finally, he looked up with relief at the sight of a train trundling ponderously into the station and struggled unsteadily to his feet.

'Come on,' Robert began to manoeuvre the wheelchair towards the train, silently hoping he wasn't going to end up stranded in the no-man's-land gap between platform and train, 'before our absence is noted at morning roll call and they send the hounds after us.'

'What are you doing? Where's this train going?' Donnie followed his companion onto the train, staring at him in confusion. 'Is this going to Hastings?'

Robert shrugged as the train began to move out of Orpington station, a montage of green flashing past as it gathered speed. 'I don't know where it's going,' he said, noting Donnie's astonished expression, 'but as you say, it'll be an adventure. We can go and look for the real Black Sabbath. And you can call me Bob.'

THE DAWN CHORUS
By A.J.R. Kinchington

<u>JAKE</u>

April 28th 2016.

He reluctantly opened his eyes.

'Are you okay in there?' a familiar voice asked.

'Sod off,' Jake muttered; anything more would have required energy he did not possess. He felt the thin, dirty blanket being removed from his face.

'Been a cold night,' the voice continued. 'Fancy some breakfast?'

Jake saw Fraser looking down at him.

'Have another look at this,' Fraser said, pushing a white paper under the blanket.

Jake knew what it said and pulled the blanket up over his head in silence. Accepting the invitation to breakfast would mean answering questions. Fraser was one of the outreach workers for Wilfred's Haven who wouldn't take no for an answer.

Awake now, Jake was shivering but knew that, if he kept still and waited for the noisy footsteps of the city workers, the shops would soon open and then light and heat would banish the chills. It seemed to take longer than usual for this to happen and his thumping headache roused him where Fraser had been mostly unsuccessful. He got up unsteadily and felt a rush of nausea grip his thin, adolescent body.

The streets surrounding Victoria Station were quiet and well lit, so anyone vaguely interested would have been able to see him, sometimes holding, sometimes leaning on the lampposts, as he slowly made his way along Victoria Street. He passed Westminster Cathedral and was momentarily aware of the dawn chorus. The beauty of their singing was lost on his solitary figure. He looked up at Big Ben and was surprised to see it was only 5:20.a.m. He crossed Westminster Bridge, noticed lights bobbing on the Thames and pushed through the doors of St. Thomas' Hospital A & E department.

The receptionist's voice seemed loud as he lied in answer to her questions. She gave him a ticket marked 16 and he sat down, avoiding eye contact with the others who were waiting. The warmth of the room took half an hour to soothe his aching head and body. The receptionist came towards him with a man in a security uniform.

'You a rough sleeper?' the guard asked.

'What's it to you?' Jake replied, shifting his feet and wondering how many times he had avoided questions.

'I'll do a check,' the guard said turning towards the receptionist as they walked away.

A woman was sitting opposite Jake, a young boy beside her. He was playing with a toy car.

Jake closed his eyes and the memory of his ten- year- old self painfully surfaced:

He had just awakened and gone to his mother's bedroom. She was asleep, the covers flung back on the empty half of the bed. Jake went to the kitchen and saw a strange man making toast and tea. He said his name was Harry and extended his hand. Jake stood still and silent. Harry picked up Jake's toy car, turned it over and suddenly threw it across the room, where it smashed into pieces.

Jake was rudely shaken by the security guard, 'You need to go to reception.'

He stumbled to the toilet, where he was immediately sick. 'Bastards!' he thought. His reflection in the mirror was pale, yet flushed, alarming him. The security guard opened the toilet door and Jake saw him in the mirror. Pushing past the guard, Jake said bitterly, 'You're all bastards.'

Leaving the hospital, he retraced his steps, knowing by the gnawing pains in his stomach and persistent hammering at his temples he would not last another night on the streets.

He stopped outside Wilfred's Haven on Wilfred Street where several men hung about waiting for eight o'clock. He stayed apart from them, but when the red door opened he followed them upstairs. Nausea from the smell of cooking bacon hit him. He sank into a seat and waited for it to pass.

Fraser noticed him and brought over a steaming plastic cup of tea. He sat next to him and together they filled out the required form.

'After you've eaten you could have a shower and get some fresh clothes. We can offer a check-up with the doctor. What do you think?'

'Yeah, I might. Cheers.'

He got up and waited in line for his bacon sandwich. It surprised him how little he could eat, since he had imagined feasting at the first opportunity. He sat down with his half- eaten sandwich and a young man, who appeared about the same age as him, sat down next to him.

'I'm Ryan. Fraser wants me to show you around.'

'Right,' was all that he could muster.

He was shown to the showers, where he allowed the hot water to cleanse and warm him. His blond hair was matted and took several washes before it lay lank and golden on his shoulders. The clothes he was offered were loose but the trainers were a good fit.

The doctor was abrupt and unemotional and gave Jake the impression he had seen it all before. To be fair, so had Jake. His symptoms, which would be registered somewhere as statistics, would contain the word homeless. The doctor bent his head, wrote quickly and said,

'Don't smoke, don't drink alcohol, don't take drugs, either smoking or intravenously, and don't have unprotected sex. You're okay but you cut it fine. Take the help.'

The doctor handed him two tablets, one for the headache and one for worms.

Returning to the main area, Jake sat for a while idly looking at the leaflets on a table and watching a breakfast show on TV. The presenters were laughing with their guests. There was something about that shared experience that made him long to see his Mum.

He remembered sitting close to her watching a comedy show when he was eleven years old:

The telephone rang in the hall and when she went to answer it, Harry came in and turned the channel to a boxing match. He told Jake that he needed to take up boxing and told him to stand up and spar with him. Harry knocked him over and then sat on him, goading him to get up. Eventually, his Mum returned and Harry laughed and ridiculed him for being a cry-baby. Later, Jake asked his Mum when his Dad was coming back but she answered sharply, 'Never ask me that again.'

He was brought back to the present when Fraser sat down beside him.

'I'm here Monday and Thursday. When you're ready we can go through some things that might help you. You don't have to do this on your own.'

Jake stood up, 'I've things to do.'

He had little experience of kindness. Bullying and rejection he knew, but kindness put him on edge. He had to be tough, strong and ruthless if he was to sort Harry out.

He left without a backward glance.

Outside in the chill April air he pulled up the collar of his jacket and noticed Ryan puffing on a cigarette. He looked smart in a black bomber jacket and dark jeans. His broad shoulders, slicked- back dark hair and wide grin gave him a jaunty air. He nodded to Jake and said,

'I come here sometimes, mostly when it's Baltic outside. What you gonna do today?' Before Jake could reply he added, 'I got places to go if you wanna tag along.'

Jake nodded and Ryan paid the bus fares to Greenwich. They were silent for most of the journey, each with his own thoughts. They had learned not to disclose any personal details. It was best to be solitary when fighting for survival. Friendships meant continuity and they lived moment to desperate moment.

The morning moved into early afternoon and so did the spring sun. It shone on their heads as they made their way through the park and onto the viewing point. Ryan climbed up onto the railings and, spreading his arms wide, began to point out the London landmarks.

'See the Gherkin? The guy at the desk gave me a note to piss off. Over there is Whitechapel, mosques and markets, easy picking there. Up there is the Jewish Jacobs, like your name. That's Canary Wharf, all suits and smart arses; they give you money to leave them alone. My kingdom, see. They all think it belongs to them but they don't know jack shit.'

His laugh was mirthless as he jumped down.

'I got some business. See you later.'

Jake wandered into the play park. It was empty, except for a young woman who was speaking into a mobile phone as she pushed a sleeping child backwards and forwards in a pushchair. He perched on the edge of a swing and scuffed his trainers across the ground. His play park in Lincoln had been quiet like this, that's why, after Dad left, he had gone there to be alone and ask God to bring his Dad back. 'Kids' stuff,' he scoffed as he pushed himself off the ground and stood up on the swing. He thought about Mum's boyfriend, Harry, and the purple and yellow 'tattoos' he made on his Mum's arms. It seemed to Jake that was about the time he stopped going to school because every lesson somehow sounded muffled.

He remembered in every excruciating detail the night before he left home:

He had arrived home at teatime, when Harry began shouting and waving a letter at him. It was from the school, stating that he had been absent for most of his final year. Harry had grabbed hold of him and began hitting him around the head, yelling at him that he was a 'bloody disgrace' and that he would march him to school in the morning. His mother was crying and pleading with Harry to stop and he did after he threw him out of the room.

Jake slid off the swing as fury rose in his chest. He stepped behind the swings and one after the other he hurled them through the air till their chains rattled and shook. The child in the pushchair began to cry and the woman shouted, 'Bloody kids!'

He wondered about Ryan, if that was his name. He didn't sound like a loser, yet he was sleeping in dirty shop doorways and was shunned by those who didn't give a damn. That prospect no longer held an attraction for him. Ten months and he was no nearer to his aim of going home to rescue his Mum from Harry. He pulled out the leaflets from his pocket that he had picked up from Wilfred's Haven and smoothed them out. He read that the charity's 'focus is to assist homeless people change their lives.' Today he had taken his first step in accepting help.

Later he walked up the hill and saw Ryan, his long legs stretched out in front of him, his head tilted back as he drank the contents of a beer can.

'Not much going on today, but here.' He handed Jake a can and a ten- pound note.

For the second time that day, Jake felt the agony of kindness. It twisted his gut and brought pain behind his eyes. He took a mouthful of beer, almost retched but swallowed hard and kept going. 'Thanks, Ryan.' Ryan looked surprised; no one used his name these days.

They lay back on the grass and closed their eyes against the warm sun. They lay in silence for a while but the banging in Jake's head made him sit up.

Below him, children had begun to fill the play park, mothers chatted over pushchairs and a crowd of boys was forming a football game. He glanced to his right and let out a 'bloody hell,' which made Ryan sit up. Rolling down the hill came two skateboards. On the first was a man in a wet suit, snorkel and flippers and on the other was a white bull terrier wearing sunglasses. They careered down the path and unceremoniously went head first into the pond. The two boys looked at each other and whooped. They rolled over and over in the soft grass, tears rolling down their faces.

In that moment a friendship was born.

CYNTHIA AND JULIE

April 28th 2016.

Soft blue light crept noiselessly up the pale silk drapes. She lay and watched as a new day made its presence known. Heavy perfume from the roses lingered in the air. All was still except for his shallow sleep-filled breathing. She would have turned and held him, but his peace would soon enough be disturbed that day. Her thoughts turned to the party last night. Friends and family had gathered to celebrate her fiftieth birthday. Marcus had filled the house with her favourite pale pink roses, which at any other time would have delighted her. Her heart sank and her head hurt, probably from a little too much wine, but it had helped to assuage the gnawing thought that had planted deep into her being.

In the late afternoon she stood at her window admiring the views down to the riverbank. Marcus was repairing the lawn and gesturing to her to come and join him, so she did.

'Cynthia, it's not too bad,' he said. The party was a great success.'

She nodded and slipped her arm around his ever-expanding waist.

'Yes, we all had a lovely evening. Our house has been such a happy place.'

Twenty-five years ago the decision to buy this large house had given them both some sleepless nights. They had been married only a year, she was pregnant and Marcus had started in a new law firm. Walton-on-Thames was near to his office in London, yet the house had a distinct country air to it, so they had taken what Marcus called 'a calculated risk.' Together they had worked at life, taken it and shaken it about until it resembled the dream of a happy, secure home for their two children. David had come along first and Lucy a slow second. They had waited five years for her and she was all the more precious for it.

They walked back up to the house, where Lucy was waiting with coffee and a plea to her Dad.

'Run me to Fraser's. He's with the outreach team tonight, so I won't be late.'

Marcus teased her a bit but, as always, he could not resist his daughter's request. Cynthia watched the pair go out hand in hand, her heart heavier than the lightness in her voice as she said,

'Bye, Darling's.'

Her mobile pinged, the message read: *hi how are you doing see you Monday it will be fine*

She did not share the optimism of the text. Indeed, she could not imagine a time when it would be fine again. How would she tell her beloved Marcus? The thought made her shudder. She looked round the room, where photographs displayed happy times. Their wedding, the children, holidays in the sun; they were all around her and her heart ached.

Two weeks ago seemed like light years away. Her fingertips had found it. The small round, squashy, hardness. Lucy had been her first thought.

*

There was nothing cheerful about the waiting room, even the pink ribbons looked forlorn. Julie looked at the poster displaying two smiling women with the positive caption 'Early Detection Will Save Your Life', but she felt anything but positive. Her worry right now was how her family would manage without her earnings. Her partner, Gary, had been his usual jokey self.

'Don't worry, babe, the kids will fetch a good few bob.' She laughed, 'Silly sod, good job I love ya.'

It was true, she did love him. Tod and Emily had been the result of their teenage passion for one another and, although money was scarce, neither of them regretted having their children. Julie's mother had helped out with childcare but her crippling rheumatoid arthritis meant that now she needed to be looked after. Julie juggled children, parents, and a job in the florist's and helped out when she could at the local church. Gary worked as a mechanic in the local garage, where his earnings – or 'living wage,' as the government called it – was barely enough to pay the rent on their flat.

She was by nature an optimist. However, at this moment in her life, sitting here in this austere place, she had to draw on her inner 'happy place' to feel a semblance of hope.

She took a well-thumbed magazine from the table and waited for her name to be called. Her attention was drawn to an older woman who looked pale and anxious. The woman kept looking at the clock on the yellowing walls and averting her eyes from the poster. Julie noted her fashionable coat and expensive shoes and wondered whether she was in the right clinic.

The woman, Cynthia, found herself sitting next to a young woman who was flipping through the pages of a magazine. Her demeanour was calm, almost nonchalant. Cynthia wondered if she was in the clinic waiting for someone; surely one so calm could not be here for the same reason she was. Her stomach and her head felt sore and her mouth was dry.

'Stuffy in 'ere. Do you want some water? I'll get us some.'

Before Cynthia could respond, the young woman went to the water cooler, brought cups back and drank noisily.

'Thank you, it is rather.'

'I'm Julie. Do you live round 'ere? I'm on Eden Street.'

'I live half an hour away, on Fairmount Avenue. Are you waiting for someone?'

Julie was surprised by her question.

'No ....Well, a miracle worker, per'aps.'

For the first time Cynthia smiled and said, 'I know what you mean.'

A nurse came and called their names. They rose together and were sent into separate rooms. Neither of them had the results they hoped for.

When Cynthia came out, Julie was talking on her mobile phone and sipping a coffee. But seeing Cynthia's ashen face, she rose, took Cynthia's arm and whispered,

'Come on. Let's get out of 'ere. The coffee tastes like shit.'

They walked to a Costa café, where Cynthia ordered a flat white. Julie ordered a Diet Coke, no glass and a straw. They sat by the window and as Julie sipped her drink, she laughingly said,

'Always have a straw. Don't want to catch anyfing nasty now, do I?'

Cynthia didn't know quite how to respond to that but replied, 'One cannot be too careful. When is your next appointment?'

'Two weeks. Monday ain't a good day for me; I'll have to get my little 'un in nursery.'

'My children are adults. My husband says I fuss over them too much.'

'What did your 'usband say about you coming 'ere today?'

'I haven't told him yet. I was waiting for my results but now I suppose…' she trailed off, looking down at her wedding ring. 'Have you?'

'It was 'im that found it. 'E always said it was me big beau'iful eyes he fell for, but 'e weren't looking at me eyes.' She glanced down to her ample breasts.

Cynthia was again taken aback at Julie's sense of humour and felt herself warming to this young woman.

'You seem so, so calm. I wish I could feel the same.'

'Well, what's the good of worrying? Mostly I put it in 'is 'ands.' She looked towards the ceiling. 'Know what I mean?'

'Mmm.'

Both fell silent for a few moments. Cynthia twisted a small signet ring with the initial C etched on it round her little finger, her shoulders hunched with anxiety.

'I 'eard the nurse call you Cynfia, is that what's on your ring?'

'No, it was my father's, Charles. He died four months ago. I wish he were still here, although being in the military most of his life he was not demonstrative. He was never really the same after Mother died. That was three years ago.' She was very near to tears, grief and the fear of her diagnosis coming in waves of despair. 'I am so sorry Julie; everything seems to have happened so quickly.'

'Yeah, I know. Me Mum says wha'ever 'appens you gotta fight it, you got kids to fink about.' Cynthia felt immediately selfish and ashamed that her thoughts had been about her own plight.

'How old are your children?'

'Tod's six, Emily's three. They're good kids.'

'How will you manage? '

'Best I can. We always do.' Julie's experience had proven that.

They sat for a while longer, talking about their proposed treatment and shared their very different background stories. Julie learned that Cynthia had studied fine art at university, where she had met Marcus. He was now a successful lawyer and she a curator in an art gallery in Chelsea. It was evident to Julie that her first impression of this tall elegant woman was correct: She was wealthy.

Julie had been born in East London. The family had been rehoused to Walton-on-Thames. She described her family as 'a bit bloody mad.' Money was always a problem to get and then to keep, yet she did not speak of it with rancour. Rather, it was something that had to be endured. However, despite their differences the one common denominator was obvious. They would share the same sense of unreality, the same prayers, the long sleepless nights and the awfulness of telling those who loved them of the fight ahead. Ordinarily, their lives would never have crossed but this was no ordinary time for either of them.

Cynthia checked the time on her stylish Gucci watch. 'I had better be going. I do hope I meet with you again. I may see you at the clinic. My appointment is on that Monday too.'

'I could give you me mobile, if you like.'

'Yes, let's keep in touch.'

Mobile numbers were exchanged, as were brief hugs as they said their goodbyes. As Cynthia waited for a cab, she watched Julie stride away in her tight jeans, trainers that lit up with her every step and her long blond ponytail swishing to and fro. A wave of tenderness for her brought tears that until now she had held back.

*

Cynthia heard the beep as Marcus locked the car. He came to her and, as usual, kissed her hello.

'Lucy and Fraser seem so well-matched. Young love, eh?'

She watched the red liquid slide into the glass and with it came the memory of the red liquid leaving her arm and sliding into the syringe. She came and sat close to him, handed him the wine glass and, steadying her voice, said:

'Marcus, I've made a new friend, Julie. I met her at Northwood Hospital.'

Something in her voice, the look in her beautiful eyes, made him take a sharp intake of breath. Her words tumbled out as she, too, tried to make sense of it all. The finding of the lump, the doctor, the clinic, the biopsy and the diagnosis.

Marcus was quiet, afraid of what he was hearing.

'Oh my God, Cyn, you did all that on your own. Why didn't you....'

'I needed to be sure before I told you. All I can think about is Lucy. She may need a scan.'

'Now you listen to me. We will get through this together.' He spoke with more conviction than he felt. 'Tomorrow we will make a plan. We will be fine.'

'That is what Julie says. She is a remarkable young woman and is facing the same situation as I am. She is so young, in her twenties with two little children.'

He gathered her up in his arms and there they sat. Fear was contagious.

*

Monday arrived and it was raining. Marcus helped Cynthia into the car.

'Please just drop me off. It's only a consultation. Lucy will be at home when I return.'

'Alright, but we need to know how best we can help with all this.' All this, seemed huge to him.

Julie's name was already being called when she walked into the clinic. With a wave, she mouthed, See you later. Costa.' Julie nodded in agreement.

Forty minutes later they were settled in Costa with their drinks.

'Well, 'ow 'ave you been? Did you tell your 'usband?'

'Yes and the children. Marcus's idea is to have a plan; he always has to find a solution to everything. David wanted to know all about my treatment and Lucy was so sweet. She held my hand and said, 'Mummy, you mustn't worry. We will get the best treatment for you.'

'Aw, that's lovely. It ain't nice telling everyone. What's 'appening now about you?'

'If the results from today are good, I will have surgery, then chemotherapy.' She instinctively stroked an imaginary hair from her forehead.

'I've been told surgery, too, but I've agreed to go on a trial of a new drug, it's specially for young women – the drug company pay a fee, so I went for it. It'll help out a bit.'

She spoke without conviction and Cynthia noticed how tired she looked.

'It's tiring being positive all the time, Julie. It can sap one's energy.'

Not that Cynthia had felt positive but she could imagine the strain of striving to constantly keep up the appearance of it.

'Yeah, I get scared sometimes.'

'As do I.' She reached out and took Julie's hand. The gesture seemed to give her permission to let the tears fall – and they did. They sat for a while longer, until they were both composed enough to leave. Outside the rain had become heavier and so, too, were their hearts.

*

Julie took her time returning home. She had so much to think about besides her treatment. Her life juggling act seemed to be spinning out of control. She thought about Cynthia and Marcus's plan – whatever that was – and wondered if she should devise one. For now, anyway, her plan was to paint a smile on her face before she went to her mother's.

'Allow love, how'd you get on?'

'Yeah, okay, yeah…'

Her mother detected a slight hesitation, so went on, 'Well me and yer Dad are gonna 'elp.' She put up a hand stopping her daughter's reply. 'No argument, girl. It's done.'

Julie knew her mother of old: What she said was gospel!

'Mum, they asked me if any of the family has 'ad cancer.'

71

'Oh, no, love, we was all 'ealfy.' Julie smiled at her Mum; apparently, rheumatoid arthritis was 'ealfy!

'I met a woman at the clinic, older than me. She's got cancer too. We 'ad a coffee an' a chat. She's a bit posh,'usbands a lawyer, got a couple of kids, but she's alright, she is.'

'Well, love, I'm glad you got someone to talk to.'

'Thanks Mum.' She said her goodbyes and felt trickles of hope that she and the family would get through the times that lay ahead.

*

Cynthia and Julie next met at Maggie's Centre. They chatted for a while about the support that they were being offered, agreeing that Maggie's was infinitely better than the starkness of the clinic where they had first met. As Julie sipped her coffee she said, 'I've been to see me boss and she's okay about me 'aving some time off.'

'That is good news; it may make things a bit easier for you. How is your treatment going, Julie?'

'Two weeks now. Bit sick in the mornings,' she said with a chuckle. 'Like bein' bleedin' pregnant again.' They both laughed.

'My surgery is next week, and then my weekly chemo will start. Marcus is taking time off to be with me.'

'Aw, that's nice. I'll see you after that. We are gonna' be fine.' She patted Cynthia's arm reassuringly.

Julie always lifted Cynthia's spirit and offered a transfusion of hope that dispelled some of the dark doubts. They said their goodbyes, hugging each other. They both knew that life would be altered in ways that would unveil itself only in the time to come.

In the car, Cynthia smiled as she thought about her young friend, her courageous optimism and her dark sense of humour.

She texted her: *I am going to fight this – even if it kills me! X*

The reply came back: *LOL x*

EPILOGUE

April 28th 2019

Five a.m. and the camera crew began silently setting up its equipment. Until then they had felt it impolite to disturb the ethereal atmosphere of the blue twilight and the singing of the dawn chorus. Greenwich Park before the Marathon had all the enchantment of a fairy-tale. Soon enough the crowds would assemble and noise would reach a crescendo as the runners and spectators spilled out to all corners of the park and the surrounding area.

Jake was showering his lean and fit body in preparation for the run. Ryan was counting – twelve, thirteen – as he did push-ups on the floor. They had become used to disciplining their bodies over the last three years.

'You know they say you shouldn't volunteer for anything, so why did you put us up for this?' Ryan asked, not really expecting a sensible answer.

'Listen, mate, it's better than 'out there,' and I'm gonna' whip your ass.'

'No chance, J.' It was said with a snort and a laugh. 'Out there' on active service in Eastern Syria – although not at the same time – they both had discovered just what their strengths amounted to.

Jake's spirits were high. With some trepidation he had been back to Lincoln to visit his mother. She had evicted her bully boyfriend, Harry, so that she had already accomplished what Jake had perceived as a rescue operation. She had agreed to come to London for a visit and they were both grateful for a new start.

Ryan was similarly in good spirits. He had found his 'family' in the army, somewhere he felt he belonged and was wanted. His leadership skills had been recognised and he was destined for a glittering career.

Not related by blood, but brothers in emotional impoverishment as youths, their bond had offered them a strong attachment and a new-found faith in their future.

*

Cynthia was putting the finishing touches to two pink tutus. Her daughter Lucy, Lucy's boyfriend Fraser, and her friend Julie were downstairs enjoying a light breakfast that Marcus had prepared. Unsurprised by the laughter coming from the kitchen, she knew Julie's comedic turn of phrase would have instigated it. The two young women had become friends during the last few years and today was the culmination of Julie and Lucy's months of training for the twenty-six-mile run. Cynthia's continuing fatigue after her treatment prohibited her from running but she contented herself in the knowledge that she and Julie were two lucky survivors.

*

It was eight a.m. and the competitors were thronging into the park. The scene was vibrant with costumes wild and varied. Live coverage would soon begin and the TV presenter was looking for people to interview. His attention was drawn to two young women dressed in pink leotards, tutus and tiaras, two young men dressed as super heroes and another in purple shorts wearing a rainbow coloured wig. Motioning to the camera crew to follow him, he joined the group.

'Morning. What are your names?'

'Julie and Lucy.'

'I see you two have Cancer Research vests on. Why is this your chosen charity?'

'See these?' Julie looked down at her breasts. 'All mine thanks to CR.'

The presenter looked a bit flustered at her reply but, recovering his composure, asked: 'And what about you, Lucy?'

'My mother, Cynthia, was my inspiration.'

'Well, I hope you have a good run today.'

Turning to the two men, he said,

'So, super heroes, you look fit. How did you train for today?'

Flexing his muscles, Ryan replied:

'Army life keeps us fit.'

'Oh, so real life super heroes?'

'Not me, mate,' said Jake, slapping Fraser on the back. 'He's the super hero.'

Fraser's purple shorts and vest had 'Wilfred's Haven' emblazoned on them, as did Jake's and Ryan's outfits.

'You three are all supporting Wilfred's Haven?'

'Yes, it's a centre of hope for the homeless in Victoria.'

'Why do you think so many turned out today?' the presenter asked.

Fraser replied: 'I think many people have already run their own personal marathon and now want to support those that are still running.'

The presenter turned to the camera, 'There we have it, viewers. Behind many of the runners today lie stories of courage and determination.'

The five friends went to their starting positions. Their energy and desire to make a difference to the lives of others spurring them on to the finishing line.

A "BUNGLAR'S" TALE
By Julia Gale

(Based on a true story!)

Joe and I were best mates, once upon a time. We had met in infant school when our fathers were in and out of prison. Both were professional felons – cat burglars, to be precise, and when I was young, I had often wondered why Dad never brought home an actual cat. As Joe and I got a little older, our fathers would take us along with them whenever they did a 'job' together. Joe lived down the road from me and our mothers became firm friends. Neither Joe nor I excelled at school as we never paid much attention to the teachers; so it was no surprise that upon leaving with only a handful of qualifications between us, we made the decision to follow in our fathers' footsteps.

Later, Joe and his mother moved to a different part of town and we stayed in contact but didn't meet up. Joe also went on to secure himself a conventional job delivering pizzas and he once sent me a photo of the trendy moped he used to get around on when he was at work. Meanwhile, I was sent on a training course in the hope that I would qualify to become a plumber. Our days of breaking and entering were over…or so I thought.

You can imagine the surprise I had when Joe rang me out of the blue one Saturday morning in January.

'Hi, Sam! Do you fancy meeting up today? I've found a new project in town – a block of flats to check out. If you like, we can work on them? You and me, just like old times. See you in an hour?'

I knew perfectly well what he was alluding to when he said that he had found a new project. This was his way of saying that he'd found somewhere that would be easy to break into. I wasn't at all keen, however, as the last time we had 'worked' on a building together, I had been arrested whilst Joe had fled before the police could catch him.

I should have said no and hung up, but it had been a while since we had seen each other and because he was my only true friend, I naively gave in to his request. Grabbing my black zip-up hooded jacket, torn jeans and the 'Yoke' trainers Mum had bought for me for ten pounds at the market, I threw them on and snatched up my backpack, without even considering taking a coat.

I felt nervous and ill at ease as I left the house. *What if he stitches me up again?* I wondered as I made my way to the bus stop. It was raining and soon the water began seeping through my trainers and the jacket afforded little protection against the January chill. Thankfully, I did not have to wait long for the bus to arrive.

When I eventually reached our agreed meeting point, it was in an area of town that I was unfamiliar with, which only increased my feelings of unease. To make matters worse, there was no sign of Joe, which was unusual as he was always very punctual. Checking my watch intermittently, I decided to take a stroll around the area to buy some cigarettes and cans of beer for courage. But, by the time I returned to the flats, Joe still hadn't arrived.

Feeling fed up with waiting and more than a little cold, I made the decision to return home; just as I was about to do so my phone began to vibrate in my back pocket. It was a message from Joe: *'I'm sorry mate but can't make it after all. I'll explain later ok?'*

The rain continued to fall and so I found shelter in the small car park outside the flats. I was still wet through and very angry with Joe, for letting me down like that. *I might as well go home,* I thought to myself. After all, there was a security door in the flats and there was not much activity passing through it; unless someone came in or out, there was no way that even a person as experienced as me would be able to enter and it was apparent that the inhabitants had decided to spend Saturday at home.

I had just turned to walk away when opportunity knocked. The security door opened and there was a young woman not much older than I struggling to get her bicycle through it. I held the door open for her and she thanked me, but I could tell that she hadn't really noticed me. She appeared preoccupied, a blank expression on her face, and I watched as she mounted her bicycle and rode away. Now that the main door was open, I was able to slip inside and remove my squelchy trainers. My clothes were still wet and clung to my body making me feel extremely cold, so I hoped, at the least, that I might be able to stand by a radiator and dry off for a while, before heading back.

With this aim in mind, I searched all the landings in the building for a radiator, but could not find any. If challenged, I knew that I could claim no purpose for being there, yet I suddenly experienced an intense surge of excitement ripple through me. My heart started to pump faster and my palms became sweaty, whilst the nervousness I had felt earlier entirely left me. My confidence restored, I knew what I must do. Just one last time, on my own. And now seemed to be the perfect chance to do it.

It was then I discovered that, in my hurry to leave the house that morning, I had forgotten to pack my lock-picking tools. *Damn it.* I tried almost every door on the ground level, but to no avail. I was about to abandon my mission –being still damp and frozen and having not eaten in a long time – when, incredibly, I found the very last door had been left unlocked! Gingerly, I crept into the flat, quietly slipped off my backpack, dropped it in the hallway and tiptoed into the living room.

It was as though I had entered a burglar's paradise. For, there on the table, a wallet lay open alongside two laptops with their memory sticks still inserted. I took up the wallet and the sticks and placed them into my pocket but the laptops, though tempting, were far too bulky to carry.

This is much too easy, I thought as I pocketed a further two items that were lying around simply waiting to be taken. Whoever lived here had been kind enough to leave a can of spray paint on the window sill, so I left a little squiggle on the wall, just to say that I had been there.

Next, I went into the kitchen, simultaneously lighting a cigarette to celebrate my success, and there I noticed a bottle of my favourite whiskey. I took a couple of swigs and checked the cupboards to see if I could find something to eat. Sure enough, it was not long before I was seated on the couch with both feet up on the table, making myself at home, eating and relishing the fact that no one had returned and caught me. I did not realise that my luck was about to run out.

At last, I decided to see what loot there was in the only other room I hadn't scouted: the bedroom. I went to the door then slowly and quietly opened it. What a shock! There sitting up in bed was a giant of a man, well over six feet tall, rubbing his eyes and staring at me. He did not look too happy.

'Who the hell are you, and what are you doing in here?!' he bellowed, heaving himself out of bed. Needless to say, I didn't stop to answer him; I was so frightened that I raced out of the building as fast as I could, leaving my backpack behind. Fortunately, he made no attempt to follow me.

I ran until I reached the town centre but a voice inside my head told me not to go home just yet so I reached for the wallet in my pocket and took out the contents: only a driving licence and some receipts, which were not of much interest. I checked it more closely and this time, hidden deeper inside, I found a twenty pound note. This was more like it. I went to tuck into a huge all-day breakfast at a nearby greasy spoon cafe.

I must have been in the cafe more than an hour before it finally occurred to me that I had left my backpack behind in the flat. I was frightened at the prospect of returning, but that bag contained things precious to me – a few photographs of Mum and Dad when they were together and my old teddy bear. Yes, strange things to carry! But I felt lost without them, so I jumped onto the next bus heading in that direction.

There was an empty police car parked on the road outside the building when I arrived. I hesitated then waited for some time but eventually I pushed open the security door, which had been left unlocked. Tentatively, I made my way back to the flat and timidly knocked. I instantly recognised the person who answered: it was the girl with the blank expression I had encountered earlier – and behind her stood the 'giant'.

'H-hi. My name's Sam and…and I've come to collect the backpack I left here earlier,' I stammered. They both stared at me in disbelief as two policemen emerged from the living room.

'Do you know this man?' one of them asked the giant.

'No, but this is the man who was in the flat earlier!' he replied.

'In that case you're coming with us,' said both the policemen in unison, barely able to refrain from laughing.

In actual fact, they laughed all the way back to the station and one of the officers even began texting his friends. 'This will make a good story for the local paper,' he told me, once he had caught his breath. I was in no mood to argue. I felt such an idiot. I sat silently in the back of the car and it was now obvious to me that I had been set up.

79

Eventually, I was allowed to go home, released on bail until further notice, and I had to walk all the way back, even though I was exhausted.

It was late when I finally arrived at the house, and I didn't expect Mum to be up, let alone that she would have a visitor. But she was, and she did.

'Hello, Sam, have you had a good day?' she called to me from the living room. I went in and before I could reply, to my horror I saw this:

There sitting on our sofa, cuddling up to my mother was Joe with a smug grin on his face.

I was so angry with them that I didn't wait for an explanation. I left, slamming the door behind me. With very little money and only the teddy in my backpack for company, I turned and fled. Where I was going, I wasn't sure, but I knew that it would be a long time before I would be able to trust anyone again.

A POST MORTEM
By Richie Stress

Everyone knows when the letterbox goes
Of the shock of the bell as the post person shows
bashed boxes, packages, plain white envelopes
Everyone knows when the letterbox goes.

Everyone knows when the letterbox goes
Of the rat-a-tat-tat when the wacky wind blows
the tat on the mat as it grows and grows
Everyone knows when the letterbox goes.

Look, a package marked **fragile:**
please handle with care
A dog shredded paper
that comes with a swear
Everyone knows when the letterbox goes.

Everyone knows when the letterbox goes
The brown falling down
A lifeline exposed.

A squiggle finger wriggle
to see what you've got
It feels like Christmas
except that it's not!

A pseudonym or alias on
leaflet spam and mailers -
now everyone knows
Everyone knows when the letterbox goes.

STARTING ALL OVER AGAIN (PART ONE): SOUL SURFING

By Janet Winson

Bill Williams folded up the solicitors' letter carefully. He turned and opened the top drawer of the grey metal filing cabinet, placing the letter behind the divider marked 'Personal' and sub-divided 'D', inserting it on top of a bulging pile of correspondence relating to his very recent divorce. He screwed up the empty envelope and threw it into the bin.

The anticipation of the Decree Nisi had totally absorbed Bill for the last couple of weeks. Twenty-five years of matrimony and four children, but now he wanted to move on. He turned to his computer and logged in. He re-filled his empty glass with more Famous Grouse from an almost empty bottle and waited for the computer to spring to life.

Maggie Wise, in the guise of 'Cookie Chick', sat in the kitchen of her small flat, in the same town as Bill's office. She was selecting a recent photograph to add to her online profile on Data Dates. A well-preserved woman of 47, Maggie was carefully choosing the most suitable photograph she could find. It had to be the one at Ginny's Hen Do, the one that was taken before she got smashed on Prosecco. She admired herself, taking in her hair with its recent colour and cut, and the favourite navy-blue dress that showed just a hint of cleavage. Her eyes looked sparkly and her wide smile natural. Inhaling noisily, she pressed the 'publish' button. Convinced that the girls at work would be proud of her as she took the first steps towards rebooting the romantic turmoil of the last eight months. She had treated herself to a total rest, however, now it was time to restart the show. She thought of Steve, the previous boyfriend who had turned out to be a complete waste of space, never in work nor paying his way. She sighed as she mentally pictured him; he had been a first-class specimen in other ways.

A period of prolonged searching on the PC every evening sometimes until the early hours followed as – in both their separate lives – Bill and Maggie spent many hours staring into computer screens, searching, filtering and admiring, sometimes laughing at a never-ending selection of photographs and personal profiles. Eventually, on a dark evening in March, while the rain was teaming down, and the wind was howling outside, Bill and 'Cookie Chick' clicked. They chose each other as 'favourites' and enjoyed some online banter for a couple of weeks.

Maggie fretted as Bill's online photograph was strictly head and shoulders, which could bring its own problems, especially with a good percentage of eligible men somewhere between overweight and obese these days. On the bright side, he claimed to be a co-owner of a very successful communications business. He stated that he enjoyed touring the continent, gourmet restaurants and classic cars. His profile name was 'World Cup Willy', which was a slight enigma until Maggie googled it and decided it was hopefully a code for his year of birth – although this would mean he was over 50 now and he was claiming to be late 40s. Wendy, Maggie's flatmate, laughed uncontrollably when Maggie told her.

'Watch out, Maggie, are you sure he is not claiming to be some sort of super-stud. The World Cup in 1966 was a long time ago!'

Maggie laughed it off. Bill looked far too respectable to even think of such a thing; however, if he was really 52 now, maybe he was dishonest and – sadly – a bit too old.

Bill and Maggie planned the first date for the Easter Bank Holiday weekend. Maggie, whose profile name was not far from the truth, hoped that if she could cut her calories drastically for the next two weeks she would squeeze quite comfortably into her favourite gypsy blouse and brand-new jeans. She was keeping options open on the cowboy boots or wedges, as this early in the year the weather could go either way.

Bill was totally blown away by Maggie's profile photograph and the hilarity of their online conversations. The very thought of meeting her had put a new spring into his step. He spoilt his two youngest sons on his contact weekend and treated them to the cinema, bowling and finishing off with giant pizzas. The boys were naturally ecstatic and arriving back home on Sunday morning made their mother instantly suspicious and borderline hostile as soon as she heard what a good time Dad had given them. She then began estimating how much Bill must have spent on them both.

Easter Saturday dawned grey and damp. Maggie found the special suede cleaner for her cowboy boots at the back of the kitchen cupboard. She stared in disbelief at her hair in the three-way bedroom mirror and after plugging the straighteners in and attempting to style her wayward blonde tresses she texted Suzy, pleading with her to come over later and sort it out. Eventually, Maggie found herself leaving London Bridge Station just before 6pm and making her way to the 'Founder's Arms' by the Thames. She felt nervous and quite sick as she approached the smoking area outside the pub, where a group of outcasts were shivering under a dismal sky that was promising a downpour any minute.

Bill spotted Maggie immediately as he had her photograph on his phone and stole many glimpses every day. His first impression was that she looked fatter and less blonde than anticipated. Maggie was still timidly looking for Bill. She could not see him and wondered if he had chickened out. When Bill tapped her on the shoulder she thought there was possibly a mistake as she was expecting a younger and much taller man. She put on her best smile, which bravely denied her deflated hopes and mentally blamed her wishful thinking on childish fantasy. Maggie and Bill had an awkward hug and were both smiling desperately. Maggie's first thought was that the cowboy boots had been a mistake and that flat pumps would have been better, Bill was barely 5' 8". Bill thought he could recognise a slight whiff of cigarettes around Maggie, despite her self-description as a 'non-smoker'. His heart dived at the thought.

'What would you like to drink, Maggie?'

Bill was trying to read her lips, as it was very noisy outside. He thought she said 'a pint' but was convinced she looked like a wine drinker so left her in a corner of the smoking area near the noisy crowd who had their drinks balanced along the wall while they dramatically recalled Chelsea's defeat and the shortcomings of the goal-keeper earlier. Bill winked at Maggie,

'I won't be long, and I'll bring the drinks out here.' It had just started to rain.

Maggie was beginning to wonder if Bill had 'done a runner' as 15 minutes passed by and the rain got heavier. Maggie seriously thought about making a hasty exit and she could now feel the rain dripping down her neck. She decided to go into the bar and look for Bill and at least get that first drink down the hatch. The area around the bar was packed and noisy. Maggie finally noticed Bill pushing through the massive queue with a pint of bitter in one hand and a small glass of white wine in the other. He had a packet of cheese and onion crisps clenched in his front teeth. He looked very nervous, Maggie suddenly felt a surge of sympathy for him. She smiled, relieved him of the pint glass and took a very large mouthful. Immediately Bill regretted buying the small glass of House White as he was now expected to drink it, whilst his pint was rapidly going down and the crisps were now in Maggie's grip.

Luckily a small round table by the door was free and within minutes Bill and Maggie were exchanging information. Maggie took a double take as Bill put his wallet into a small 'man bag' that he had hanging over his shoulder. Her heart sank for a second time and right down into her cowboy boots. It was her personal opinion that real men owned scruffy little wallets, and that 'man bags' were a vanity. However, as the minutes ticked into an hour, Bill would not let Maggie go to the bar and although he decided to stick with the wine, just to keep face, he bought himself large glasses of Chablis.

Over a couple of rounds, the atmosphere slowly mellowed and they moved on to discuss the bar menu. Maggie now took a good long look at Bill, noticing the expensive cabled jumper and well-fitting trousers. He certainly had office worker's hands, not a broken nail or callous to be seen. Now on his third glass of wine, Bill started to wonder why Maggie was still single. He realised that she exuded an overwhelmingly delicious scent and was quickly seduced by her low, slightly husky voice and ready giggle. While sharing the menu, their hands met for a few moments. Maggie was now on half-pints and Bill was relieved, a woman with a pint glass was a complete turn off for him. His mother and ex-wife were both extremely genteel ladies, and so drinks were taken slowly and sparingly.

It took ages for the waitress to notice them and take the order. A large oversized cocktail shaker full of frites arrived first. When the meals arrived shortly afterwards, Bill's eyes greedily rested on

Maggie's generous mixed grill, making his vegetable moussaka appear bland in comparison. He went back to the bar to demand some proper black pepper. As the surfeit of best bitter wove its magic, Maggie was beginning to feel increasingly sorry for Bill. The fact that he referred to his ex-wife as the 'Wicked Witch' had been off-putting to begin with, yet the food and alcohol were fast taking the edge off any distractions. Maggie racked her brains to try and remember if her flatmate was planning on coming home later.

The food had been consumed and the plates remained on the table, the grease was beginning to congeal. Bill started to glance at his watch and was becoming restless, drinking the dregs of his wineglass with a sense of finality. Maggie took a chance and putting her head to one side, almost on Bill's shoulder, she whispered into his ear,

'Do you want to come back to Clapham with me later? Wendy's away in Brighton until Monday. We could have a nightcap together and maybe watch something on Netflix?' She immediately realised she had overstepped the mark as Bill was not looking at her but gazing over her left shoulder.

'Thing is, Mags, my youngest, Tom, is singing in the church choir for the Easter Service in the morning. I've promised to be there and it's an early start. He has a solo, so it's a big day for him. First time he's been chosen for a solo, he's got a lovely voice, I feel quite nervous for him to be honest.'

'That's ok', said Maggie feeling thoroughly embarrassed, blushing hard, her cheeks flaming as if she had eaten a double strength Vindaloo.

The goodbyes took place on the concourse at London Bridge Station where Bill had to run to catch his fast train home. They clung together for a couple of seconds as Bill whispered in her ear.

'I'll ring you on your mobile, Tuesday lunchtime, is that ok?' They shared a hasty, alcohol-inspired kiss that promised nothing.

Bill fell asleep on the train and nearly missed his stop. His mind was racing, despite – although probably due to – the whole bottle of Chablis. He realised that he was very attracted to Maggie; however, the reality of paternal responsibilities painfully attacked his brain like pins in a pincushion. Bill's grip on reality was ebbing away as he started to wish that Maggie had been on the scene years before the difficult yet comfortable burden of family life had changed him. After a reasonably long and sobering walk to his new apartment, any shreds of fantasy had disappeared. Reality hit as he entered the dark living room with all the ambience of an IKEA showroom. He found the light switch and his eyes fell on the school photos of the boys, lined up on a light oak bookshelf. Standing a little apart from these was the last photograph he had of Helen. It was her graduation photograph where her golden hair shone in the sun and tumbled down in loose curls, contrasting with her dark academic robes. Bill quickly turned into the kitchen and found the opened bottle of Jack Daniels that he knew would drown the thoughts that were beginning to choke him. Oblivion was his goal most nights.

Maggie was now back in her flat in Clapham and feeling disappointed and extremely lonely. She realised that some ketchup had spilt right down the front of her gypsy blouse. She went into the bedroom and quickly took off everything, the boots were kicked off and landed by the chest of drawers. She grabbed her comfy, fleecy, pink dressing gown that had the word 'Princess' embroidered on the back. She routinely looked at her laptop to see if there were any new matches from the dating site. One new match was highlighted and as she scrolled up, the image of a very hairy and unkempt man appeared. The fact that this was obviously the best photograph that he could find almost made her laugh. She pressed 'delete' and signed out. After closing her lap top, she searched for the half-bottle of supermarket vodka, cursing softly until she found a bottle of tonic in the fridge, hidden behind a forgotten, half-eaten pizza.

STARTING ALL OVER AGAIN (PART TWO): TRAWLING THE CATCH

By Janet Winson

Maggie Wise was tossing and turning in her sleep, pummelling her pillows. She had the sensation of sliding down further and further until she was deafened by the harsh sound of church bells ringing. In front of her, she was aware of a small fair-haired choirboy in a halo of bright sunshine. His perfect high notes soared like a lark. Suddenly she recognised Bill Williams, who was watching the boy as he sat with his wife and family in the front pew. The vision changed into a table heaving with a huge leg of lamb and tureens of steaming vegetables, accompanied by the smell of meaty gravy, which she could see was oddly contained in one half of a chocolate Easter egg.

Suddenly wide awake, Maggie shot out of the bed as the bile rose in her throat, she ran to the bathroom and threw up the contents of her churning stomach. She thanked her lucky stars that she had made it in time and rested her head against the cold shower screen. Memories of the night before came to her in colourful vignettes making her shudder with embarrassment. Despite all her careful planning, she had made such a fool of herself. The bottle of vodka was finished and she felt terrible. She wondered what Bill was thinking now and resigned herself to never hearing from him again.

*

Bill was dropping his former wife and two younger sons back at the large detached house in Kent, which was now owned solely by his ex-wife, Judith.

'Happy Easter, boys. Don't make yourselves ill on all those Easter eggs'. Only Tom, the youngest, waited long enough to reply.

'Thanks for coming to the service, Dad. I'll miss you today, Easter won't be the same this year. Have you got time to take me to the park tomorrow to practice goal kicks?'

Bill felt his eyes automatically prickle and his throat contracted. Every single parting was still painful.

'Sure thing, Tom. I'll text you tomorrow morning. Love you, son!'

Bill arrived back home at his small apartment. He sadly assessed the state of the food in his small larder fridge and then opened his tiny countertop freezer, dragging out a box of cod in parsley sauce. He needed to eat but wasn't hungry. This morning he realised how much he regretted the way he had treated Maggie last night. He had been cruel and dismissive of her totally spontaneous offer of a "nightcap", which must have taken a lot of guts. He felt small and mean in belittling her and wanted to make amends. He found his mobile phone and scrolled down his contacts list.

*

Maggie jumped out of her skin as her mobile began to vibrate to the sound of the Beach Boys. Good Vibrations, indeed! Maggie had settled back to bed and taken some paracetamol. She grabbed her phone and pressed the green button, barely awake and not recognising Bill's number.

'Hi, Maggie. It's me, Bill here. Are you ok? I'm so sorry about the way I charged off last night. I want to make it up to you. Are you free next weekend. It will be fine as Judith is taking all three boys to Wales to visit her sister. Please say yes, Maggie'. It was a very lengthy speech, delivered hastily, with a dry throat and a racing pulse.

Maggie was in a state of confusion as she had not expected to hear any more from Bill. Her own voice sounded like somebody else's and she came across very bright and clear.

"I'd love that, Bill. Please don't worry about last night. It was my fault; I was presuming too much. How could you let your son down?"

"That's very gracious of you, Maggie. I don't deserve it. Is there somewhere you'd really like to go? We can spend a whole day and into the evening". He stopped abruptly and anxiously awaited her answer. He said quietly, 'You choose, Maggie.'

'I love rivers, old buildings; how's that for a start? Anywhere out of the smoke really. Yes, I'd love that'.

The second date was arranged there and then. Bill and Maggie were both astounded that it had happened so easily.

Bill collected Maggie in his comfortable Range Rover from outside her flat in Clapham. They took the South Circular towards Kent. Maggie felt happy and relaxed; she had decided to dress down today in navy trousers and an old denim jacket. She didn't really want to wear her trainers but realised they were the obvious choice for a day out in late April.

Once settled in Bill's Range Rover, they listened to Radio 2 and ate Mint Imperials all the way to Rochester. Bill thought how lovely Maggie looked, stealing a sideways glance at her. He was aware of the need to treat her with great care today and make her feel special. He regretted his previous thoughtlessness and felt amazed at his luck that she had generously given him this second chance.

Bill had chosen Rochester for their day out. It was where he had grown up and been educated. He knew every square inch of the area and most of its history. He found a parking space on the Promenade Road overlooking the River Medway. They took a leisurely walk up the steep hill towards the Castle walls and he steered her into a nearby Café adjacent to the Cathedral for a coffee. It was still early and not yet busy in the High Street. They sat side-by-side and gazed out through the diamond-paned window. He again admired her unusual hazel eyes and lightly made-up face. Maggie smiled and was very attentive, Bill realised he was falling for her. He couldn't help himself.

'I've been here before!' Maggie grabbed Bill's arm as they left the café. Bill wondered what she meant, but Maggie continued excitedly, tripping over her words in excitement.

'I came here on a school trip years ago. We were reading "Great Expectations" for English Literature GCE. We were exploring the town and its connections. I remember that one of the shops had a model of Miss Havisham's Bride Cake and Wedding Feast. There was a fake rat on the top tier, eating the icing!'

'I know where the original Satis House actually is, just up behind the Cathedral. Let's take a look!' said Bill. They continued up the High Street, laughing at the names of shops and cafes, Pip's Parlour, Magwitch Treasures, Estelle's Hair and Beauty, and the two blue plaques near the Post Office. Maggie was impressed with Bill's knowledge and enthusiasm. She put her arm through his and they walked the cobbled streets around The Vines. Bill explained that this was where the monks had tended their grapes centuries ago when they lived as a community around the early cathedral. They did not stop talking until they had walked a full circle arriving back at the great doors of the cathedral; Bill held the door as Maggie entered.

'I was a Chorister here thirty years ago, Maggie. I studied at The King's School that we passed earlier. I suppose that's why Tom's solo on Easter Sunday was so important to me. He takes after me more than my other children. He loves music just as I did, back when life was so simple. I'm lucky to have such wonderful memories from my childhood here that I can recall when life is getting me down. It's like a medicine for me'.

They sat down on a pew near the back and Maggie looked all around her, silently absorbing the atmosphere of the great Cathedral: its jewel-like windows and enveloping quietness and the memorials to the great and good. She felt calm until she was disturbed by a sudden flashback to her own upbringing and her secondary education at the Convent of The Good Shepherd. She tried in vain to stop those thoughts but the dark, closed memories flashed up once again. The memory she had put to the back of her consciousness for thirty years was hitting her hard, and, as always, it was hurting and tears felt very close. She worked hard at keeping herself steady and concentrating on anything she could find to distract her. Bill unexpectedly stood up and walked towards a side chapel. He was feeling in his pocket, presumably, for coins. She got up and slowly followed him.

She saw him standing in front of a triple row of tea-light holders, most of them supporting a small, golden, winking flame. The flames burned brightly and were pointing up towards the mighty, embossed ceiling, highlighting the corners of the dark chapel with its flowers and prayer books. Bill was placing a new, unlit tea-light into a holder on the top row. He lit it from the flame of its neighbour. He walked back slowly and watched this new flame flicker and strengthen.

Bill took Maggie's hand and led her back towards the quiet corner where they had been. Bill's face looked sad and troubled.

'I think I need to tell you about Helen, Maggie. It's only fair that you know.'

Bill saw the apprehension in Maggie's hazel eyes, already slightly wet. He continued to speak, although his voice was quiet and different from the one she felt she knew.

'We lost our eldest child, Helen, our only daughter, five years ago. She became ill the day after her graduation ceremony at University with meningitis. We never said goodbye. She was already in a coma by the time we drove up the motorway. Her mother and I were already having problems in our marriage and couldn't support each other through that terrible year. We were both so unhappy but had nothing left to give to each other'.

Maggie searched for some tissues in her cavernous navy-blue bag and then put her arm round Bill's shoulders. They sat like that for some time. Maggie's thoughts wandered to the first and last time she had seen her own tiny, new-born daughter, already promised to new parents before she had even been given a name. At the age of seventeen, she had barely been considered in the whole episode. The "gymslip pregnancy" mortified her parents and was slickly concealed and remedied by a convent full of nuns. Maggie had found her first, early experience of love a dangerous and painful experience. Nothing had happened over the following years to change her view, although she still held out a shaky glimmer – a possibility of hope. This memory was tightly concealed in what felt like a lead-lined compartment somewhere below her heart. She had accepted that it would stay in place there, possibly into old age, and probably death.

Bill and Maggie left the Cathedral after a while, then wandered back along the High Street. They didn't talk very much but something had gelled between them. They took their time strolling around the exterior of the Castle, enjoying the spring daffodils and the mild sunshine. Families were in abundance: boys and girls on bikes and scooters, toddlers taking early steps with doting parents and the usual fresh season of new baby buggies with proud but nervous owners. Maggie felt different somehow. Bill's honesty earlier had released so much emotion in her that she yearned to share her own sad story and she felt she had possibly met someone she could trust now.

I've really enjoyed today. Thank you, Maggie, you've been such great company". Bill opened the car door for Maggie and helped her into her seat.

"Where shall we go next?" Maggie turned to Bill as he started the engine and smiled at him. This new man in her life was real and three dimensional. None of the little upsets of the day had mattered. The lipstick that fell out of her bag and rolled away in the dark of the cathedral, the coffee that she had managed to spill all over her jacket, the realisation that she had not put a comb in her handbag. These were ordinary things that could have easily spoiled a whole day for her in the past. Instead, she felt a lightness from the possibility of sharing her heavy burden and feeling completely happy all over, body, mind, and soul. Maggie had always known that the missing link in her life chain could be repaired by someone very special. At last she felt a vestige of hope.

Bill also felt a lightness in himself. He drove on up the hill towards the railway bridge, taking the road back and joining the busy Saturday afternoon traffic. It felt amazing to have Maggie just sitting there beside him.

THE SLOTH
By Glynne Covell

I am a sloth or sometimes known as SLOATH
Whatever you fancy,
I answer to both.

But why am I so slow you say…
It's down to low grade leaves and such
And, really, I'd have it no other way:
I enjoy the leaves so much!

When I'm awake, I hang upside down
And sometimes slowly crawl.
My toes are strong and grip so well
That never do I fall!

I'm a three toed sloth by the way,
Friendly and kind to all I meet
But beware my cousins with just two toes
Dangerous are they; consider them foes!

I spend most of my day asleep you know
Up to twenty hours of rest!
But when I'm awake
I really go for life,
Give it my absolute best!

I move so slowly, it gives me time
To think, to dream and plan
Oh, it's a hard life being a sloth, you know
But I do what I want, when I can.

I can turn my head 270 degrees
It's like having eyes in the back of my head

Not quite as good as an owl, I guess
but useful when hanging about instead.

My back legs hardly work at all
Unless I'm swimming in water
Then they're three times faster
And never do they falter!

But here's the rub I ponder on
That maybe it's man who's got it so wrong
It's not the sloth who's slow
But man who is fast
A question as broad as it's long.

LIGHTHOUSE EDDY
By C.G. Harris

It is a truth well acknowledged in my country that fact is stranger than fiction; I care to believe that this wisdom stands true the world over.

I've travelled much, both believing and disbelieving the things I had seen. I have been often elated and sometimes disturbed. Run the gauntlet between truth and lies as you read and make of my story what you will – only know that I insist it happened just as I relate, and that I wish it had not.

To call your country and the things in it *quaint* does it a great disservice. The lighthouse at Spirren Head was not quaint; the narrow sand spit on which it lay, reaching out into an austere North Sea and curling back like a beckoning finger into the Humber estuary, even less so. I wondered what my countrymen in cosmopolitan Boston, Massachusetts, USA, would call this bleak place, and I guessed quaint would not be the word that they would use – no sir.

That being said, I reckon that all lighthouses, by their nature, brooding constantly as they do over scenes of potential and actual tragedy, will always have a melancholic air. I did not hold its bleakness against it; I merely looked across the bay and felt a compulsion to look out from those rocks to where a surly sea and sky merged with a darkening acceptance of the early dusk.

To this end, I made my way on foot through the village of Essingham, which was a single, unlit street with cramped, glowering houses on either side and the sole feature of redemption being a public house just lighting up; you can bet that I had it in mind to call in when I came back that way.

I found the spit was a combination of sand and shingle, at times narrowing to 50 yards across with mudflats on the landward side; the occasional gull rose and twisted in the wind, and I, in turn, stepped out and braced myself against it, suddenly chilled and wondering why the lighthouse remained unlit.

It was three miles to the southernmost tip, far enough to call it lonely, if not outright isolated. When I reached the base of the lighthouse, it was what we call a damp squib, the door and all windows boarded. Quite evidently, it was no longer in use – I took a turn around it all the same, and on the seaward side, a moon, half-hearted until now, spilled light through the length of its column, such that my shadow was cast against grainy, flaking walls, elongated and distorted.

A small wooden structure stood to the side, which, by its design, looked as though it might once just have housed an occupant or two; the whole prospect became suddenly grim to my writer's mind. The dark, defunct tower stretched into the night sky in such a forlorn manner, its railed apex shrouded on one side by shadow and the other by moonlight, that I suddenly felt the need for company, and I would take my chances on whether that was yet another cheerless Yorkshireman; despite the darkening, intermittent cloud, I made my way back along the spit more hurriedly than I had come.

The Wayfarer was the kind of public house that delights us Americans, a kind of a throwback to pre-*bistro* days, not quite with sawdust on the floor but quiet, apart from a fizzing fire, and with an assortment of ales with unlikely names like *Red Gander* and *Winter Mist.* I strode to the bar with relief, removing my rucksack whilst ordering the latter ale – it seemed to suit both the mood of the district and the inclement weather, and I was pleasantly surprised to find the barman smiling as he served me. In an arch manner, he asked me if I had been to see the lighthouse.

"Why, yes I have. How do you know? Is it a Yorkshire knack to read minds?"

"Now't else to see round here. You will have heard all about it of course…?"

"I can see that it is out of use, is there a story behind that? Stories are my stock-in-trade."

"Aye, there's a story." He glanced towards the fireplace. "I have some barrels to change; then, if you've still a mind, I'll settle your curiosity. It'll not be throng tonight."

I nodded and raised my glass, and he wandered towards the cellar door while I looked around for a comfortable seat. Being the only patron, I had the fairest of choices, and I well liked the look of a high-back chair in a dark corner near the fire where the shadows flickered in and out in a lively fashion. It was only when I got closer and my eyes adjusted to the gloom that I noticed the man. He leaned forward as if he had detached himself from the fabric of the chair opposite mine.

"You American?"

"Yes sir, I am."

"I'm not keen on Americans."

This was more like the type of welcome I was familiar with, and so, not taken aback, I sat and said that I was sorry to hear that and continued in a friendly manner.

"Well, I'm guessing you are a local man, so I'm pleased to meet you at any rate. The landlord has promised to give me a little of the local history."

"If you mean the lighthouse, there's only one man to speak with" and he lifted his chin. "I was the last keeper at Spirren Head."

This was the kind of *horse's mouth* information that I adored, and I adjured him to continue, the while pulling out a notebook that had seen better days but was, at that moment, filled with the precious observances of my itinerancy.

He nodded at the notebook. "You can write this down... *I killed my wife.*"

I guess you could say that this was not quite what I expected to hear, but he continued unconcerned and said again, "Write it down, man."

I studied his face, and though his eyes had a stagnant look about them, I somehow did not disbelieve him. His face had gathered together over the years into a middle-aged rigidity of stoicism; it was not a cruel face – but there was about the lips a suggestion that this could be a hard man, and I did not doubt that, whether by accident or with aforethought, it was entirely possible. I wrote, *A man killed his wife,* and he nodded when he saw what I had written.

"I didn't hate her. 'Eck, I loved her. But I couldn't let her go, not after all those years."

I have learned that silence is the writer's tool when someone is either confessing or speaking from the heart; so, though I was taken aback, I kept my head down and scribbled as he spoke.

"My wife's name were Isolda. It's Welsh, meaning *fair*. And she were. Edward, Eddy as is, and Isolda. We grew up in Killensea where there's now't to do but cling to the things that give you pleasure and hope and that were each other. As young tykes, we were content well

98

enough, and we sort of fell into marriage; to me it seemed natural, but as we got older... I were always afraid that she wanted more." He nodded several times.

"We both loved the sea, and when the keeper's job came up, we took it; we both regretted it. I could see from the moment we moved in how restless she were. She were still affectionate and always swore she loved me, but I knew well she were bored and unhappy, and in my frustration, I became spiteful. I'll admit that." He paused. "And then *he* came along."

I looked up. I guess I could see somewhat where this was leading, and I wondered how many times this had played out in the course of human life, with all its frailties and jealousies.

"He were American too." He leaned over and looked closely at my face; I was starting to feel uncomfortable when he sat back and continued.

"It takes at least three keepers to run a lighthouse, did you know that?"

"I didn't realise that, no."

"Aye, we struggled along for months with only the wind and the sea for company when I was told that they'd found another keeper at last. It's usual for another family to come in, but a job like that is hard to fill. My chest hurt when I saw how she looked at him, though he were pleasant enough and didn't seem to notice. Adam was a traveller, and I knew he wouldn't stick to a job such as ours for long. But he was young and adventurous, and if her head needed turning even more, he were the one to do it. I didn't believe half his tales but she did. She imagined all that she had missed, and she were right of course."

He looked down at his empty glass, and I glanced round at the bar with a view to offering him a drink. In my fascination, I had not noticed but the pub had filled somewhat despite the landlord's expectation. Before I could speak, however, he continued, and his words were heavy, whether loaded with guilt or sorrow I could not say.

"He stayed longer than I thought or wanted and made himself quite at home in the settlement while we lived inside. And every day I were looking for a sign of anything but a friendship between them. I saw nothing, but still I felt pieces of her slipping away from me while I boiled inside." He paused. "Then I saw it, just a touch of the hand but it were enough…"

The flames made his eyes dance, and I began to see what jealousy might do to a man, however decent they might once have been.

"I had a quiet word with him, I told him I wanted him gone that night. He said nothing but looked at me as if I were cracked, and that made the blood boil in my veins… that evening I brought Isolda here to this pub. It were busy just like it is now, and we sat here in these very seats. I told her that Adam was going away, would be gone by the time we returned."

He rubbed a hand across his face which had begun to look strained and with a certain wildness ebbing and flowing across it, as if taking on the features of that tempestuous sea he had guarded against.

"As soon as I told her, I knew I had been right to get rid. I'm not saying anything happened, but she had been unfaithful in spirit if not in the flesh; I'm not sure which is worse. I've a mind it wasn't even Adam but all that he represented that brought her discontentment to the fore; she got up with her hand over her mouth and sat in that chair over there in the corner, staring at me… then she ran to the door, hoping to see him one more time, I'm thinking."

I looked around at the now crowded pub and saw another high-back chair opposite where there now sat a pretty, yet pallid-faced and worn woman with dark hair, ill-defined against the backdrop, looking at her hands folded on the table.

"Where that lady is sitting?"

He sat stock still and stared into the uneven light.

"Where, man, where?" he lowered his voice, and I could hardly hear him above the stirred-up chatter of the locals.

"Why, there sir, right there."

He leaned towards me, almost as if for comfort, but looked hard over my shoulder, his eyes widening.

"What is she doing?" he whispered into my ear.

I glanced around in embarrassment. "She… she is looking at us…" and I felt coldness at the back of my neck as I said this, despite the heat of the fire.

"Is she by God?" he whispered again.

"It's alright, sir, she is leaving."

"IS SHE BY GOD?!!!" he roared and leapt to his feet.

I could not help but leap to my feet also and sent my chair crashing backwards in shock. With a rush to the door, Eddy was gone whilst the solid Yorkshire patrons were silenced; I guess that I reinforced their belief that strangers among them were not a thing to be encouraged. I kept my head down and hurriedly followed; do not ask me why, for I am unable to provide an answer unless it be that my appetite for the macabre, for truth and resolution, have always compelled me in that way.

A north-easterly wind had picked up and chilled the winter evening yet more with its vigour and the moon had risen, low yet large and round, and by its light I could see two figures in shadowed profile ahead. The one hurried with a woman's bearing, one hand now holding a shawl that kept her long, dark hair in place, whilst the man was in all furious urgency following but still several dozen paces behind.

Do you know, try as I might to keep them in view, each time I looked they were further away, scurrying in fear and anger along the wind-blown spit until they were diminutive figures, and I beat my way through the spray that flew at me from the greasy rocks in a bid to keep them in sight.

I was aware that the tide was seeping across the narrowest part of the spit, threatening to cut me adrift from the mainland, and I was ready to turn back when something occurred that set the hackles on my neck rising. The lighthouse beam came on! It slashed through the night sky, and the surrounding darkness withdrew before it; it was a solid spear of light that may once have saved souls but to me was now just a beacon that drew me towards it in awful fascination.

I finally came near it, wet, shaking with cold and a kind of apprehension, and I made out the figure of the woman leaving the settlement's nearest abode. To me, it seemed as though she had both her hands to her head as if tearing her hair, and I guess the moaning could have been the wind or that of a woman who had lost something that she never really had; she ran into the lighthouse, and the man called Eddy followed her deliberately and slowly.

I do not know what I expected or even why I was there, but I stood, sodden, frozen, while the wind churned white sprays into my eyes and whipped and eddied around me, locking me there, the lighthouse in front and the open door of the settlement behind; I slowly raised my head and could imagine one figure flying in circular haste to the

101

pinnacle of that tower whilst the other followed with a measured tread, whether to harm or entreat I do not know.

There are some things I will never forget. Two figures appeared, swaying, locked together, crashing against the summit rails with a stream of light surrounding them, no longer sharp and straight but vaporous and clinging. If anything, the woman fought the harder, and her hands and arms beat down repeatedly while the man gripped her, it seemed desperately, until, with a cry, the woman fell – a black shape tore downwards and was dashed on the sea-hewn rocks before me.

I wanted to scream, I remember that. I wanted to scream, but the whole of me was locked in a kind of frozen terror that would not release me from its hold. Only when I forced myself to look away from that twisted form and looked upwards to see Eddy pointing a finger at me could I speak, and it was to whisper to myself repeatedly "oh Christ, oh Christ, oh Christ…" and when I saw Eddy mouth "YOU!" I ran.

I'm not ashamed to say that I ran, even though I was not exactly sure of what I had seen. I ran because Eddy had pointed at me, and his eyes were red. Mostly, I ran because Eddy did not like Americans; he had told me so himself.

I slipped and slid and stumbled my way along that spit and waded through the incoming tide with the lights of *The Wayfarer* signalling safety and a harbour within which to save myself and my sanity, perhaps. When I, at last, reeled through the door, it was into a deserted pub, and the landlord stood there in sane mundanity wiping glasses behind the bar.

He looked at me in astonishment." Good God man, what's happened to you?!"

"Give me something stronger than *Winter Mist,* and I'll tell you."

He quickly drew me a double measure of Scotch, which had me coughing, and we sat (I insisted that it was not in that corner by the fire), and when I had finished and had begun to think straight, I said we should call the police. He looked at me hard and said –

"I don't think so… Eddy has been dead these last eight years."

I kept silent.

"Killed his wife, threw her from the top of the lighthouse, but not before she stabbed him first."

"But you must have seen him! And everybody else too!"

"Not been a soul in all night." He gave a bleak laugh. "Unless you count Eddy's, of course."

"What happened to Adam, for God's sake?"

He rubbed his chin. "Well, some say he just upped and left, and others that Eddy lost his temper with him... no one has seen him since."

"Can you believe what I say?"

He raised his eyebrows in that slow, Yorkshire way and said –

"Looking at you, man, no one would doubt it."

So, there you have it. That good landlord bid me stay overnight and a few more days on top, free and gratis; I'll never think badly of a Yorkshireman again, unless he happens to be a lighthouse keeper.

For myself, why, I am finding Boston, Massachusetts, USA, good and honest and safe, which is how I like things now, though I sometimes lie in my bed and wonder with awfulness, and not a little pity, about those two souls grappling on the edge of eternity *for* eternity... and I consider that, though I am a proud American, that night on the Head was the one occasion I did *not* want to be such, no sir.

As for my friends, well, I think they may well have laughed and shaken their heads at my tale were it not for the fact that I returned with my hair sheer white. In consequence, and in deference to me I guess, I have heard none of them call England quaint anymore.

This story was first published October 2017 in 'Light and Dark: 21 Short Stories' by C.G. Harris, which was shortlisted for the Georgina Hawtrey-Woore Award 2018 for Independent Authors. Book available on Amazon.

SMALL BEGINNINGS
By Tony Ormerod

'Why don't you just do as you're told?' The Sergeant, overweight and red-faced with anger, was at the end of his tether. This upstart, this foreigner, this peculiar-looking man who reminded him so much of what's-his-name, that bloke in the funny American films that he used to watch before the war, had once again questioned his authority. The two men stood barely a metre apart, glaring at each other.

'May I remind you, Sergeant, that I didn't join up to peel potatoes?'

'Tell me then, Private, why did you join up in this army anyway? You should be fighting with the Austrians in Italy or Russia or anywhere else. In any case, as far away from me as possible.'

'Does it matter? I should be fighting the Frogs and the Tommies for the glory of the Aryan race. That is where the action is!' He waved his potato peeler in the general direction of the front, annoying the older man intensely.

'Never mind all that nonsense, you should thank your lucky stars that you work in this field kitchen. The grub may be lousy, but at least you can survive.' The Sergeant, a Regular soldier, looked towards the booming of the big guns before adding, 'that is, if you don't die of bloody food poisoning. Now get on with these spuds or I'll have you for insubordination.'

'Damn these potatoes and damn you, this is no job for a warrior.' Peevishly, he threw down the peeler and tore off the (rather fetching) pinafore which his mother had sent by post a couple of days earlier.

'I'm giving you your last warning,' the Sergeant prodded the Private's chest with a chubby finger. 'Either you do as you're told or you're on a charge.'

'What's going on here Sergeant?' They had not noticed the Lieutenant who had arrived in time to hear the final warning. The Sergeant and the Private snapped to attention as he confronted them and, as one, they saluted the senior officer, who returned the compliment with a salute that was half dismissive, half weary.

'It's this man, Sir, this man is insubordinate, Sir.'

'I have just the job for him.' said the officer, holding up a languid hand that seemed to signal his indifference to the Sergeant's problem.

'You,' he continued, pointing at the Private who stepped forward smartly before coming to attention and saluting again. 'I have an important but not too dangerous job for you.' He waited for some sort of reply, but none came. There was something odd, something distasteful about the little man that offended his Prussian officer's sensibilities.

'Can you run, Private?'

'Yes Sir.'

'Can you run fast, Private? Because I want you to deliver this message to the front line — and it's urgent. Our gallant lads are to be relieved and replaced. You will have the privilege of bringing some good news.'

'You can count on me, Lieutenant.'

'Good man, take this message and run like hell to our defensive positions, find the Commanding Officer and deliver it.'

The Private accepted the proffered envelope with alacrity, saluted yet again, and had half turned when he was restrained by one of the officer's arms.

'By the way, Private, succeed in this mission and there may be a stripe or two in it for you.'

The Lieutenant and the Sergeant watched as the soldier quickly disappeared into the distance.

'Excuse me, Sir, permission to speak freely, Sir?' The Sergeant did not wait for a reply.

'May I just say, Sir, that I'm surprised you've given that insolent dog an excuse to dodge the column? How can I maintain discipline dealing with other ranks when you make promises to promote the likes of him?'

'Sergeant, calm down, it's doubtful you'll have to worry about that particular Private anymore.'

'What do you mean, Sir?'

'I mean that he won't be back.' The Lieutenant extracted an expensive silver case from his tunic, opened it and offered a cigarette. 'The German army can do without his sort, Sergeant, don't you agree?'

'Well I suppose so, Sir, but didn't you say that the mission was not too dangerous?'

'I lied, Sergeant'. The officer lit his own cigarette, drew heavily on it, and blew out two perfect smoke rings.

'How… how do you…*what* do you know, Sir?' The Sergeant marvelled at the cold bloodedness of it. 'Typical bloody Prussian,' he thought.

'We captured a French infantryman a couple of hours ago. It turned out that his speciality was laying down poison gas and, after a little persuasion, he told us the exact time that the next attack is due. Naturally, I've alerted everyone at the front, and they've withdrawn of course. Your friend will arrive just as the show begins.'

'But the message, Sir?'

'It was my laundry bill.'

Approximately half a kilometre away, the Private hastened towards the front. Unusually quiet at that moment, it nevertheless was where the action was, and he was elated at the thought of his mission. 'At last,' he thought, 'something worthwhile, something that would show a bullying Sergeant and a pompous Prussian that I am a man to be reckoned with.' After this runner role he would, he hoped, be shortly in a position to order people around himself with his one stripe, or maybe two? An Iron Cross perhaps? Spurred on, he began to run faster. He had convinced himself that one day the whole world would hear from Adolf Hitler.

CONNECTION LOST
By Jan Brown

Megan Powell tried to hug the cold away. Her threadlike skin was mottled with blotchy brown moles and stringy blue veins. She had downloaded her notice of termination that morning. Not surprising considering her lacklustre performance over the past few years. She had kept a low profile and failed to reach many of her targets, but she had hoped her previous exemplary record might allow for a possible extension.

'You've done a better job than anyone else I know,' Carmen assured her friend as they sat together in Megan's city apartment. Her bifocals balanced at the very edge of her outstanding nose. 'You've had to work with all the losers, wasters, and whiners.' Carmen's chest expanded as she gathered momentum. 'Teenage yobs, drug addicts, and alcoholics.' She paused, struggling for other appropriate nouns, and then slowly deflated.

Megan sank back onto the sofa, feeling suddenly exhausted and alone. 'But many exiteers didn't stand a chance after their parents were terminated, and with schools closed down or redefined as production hubs, they had no one to help them set goals or develop their productivity.' She stared bleakly at her friend.

Carmen's bifocals glittered, and her vision obscured as she leaned forward. 'Surely you must see your role in the CEU as your greatest achievement?'

'I don't know, Carmen. People don't seem to be very nice anymore; everyone just looks after their own interests.'

The Certificate of Exceptional Usefulness (CEU) 1.1.0 was a popular government initiative which took its early inspiration from the hysterical Boxing Day crowds that gathered to get a cheap widescreen TV or sofa. People would literally kill to get hold of these precious things. These days it was all about targets; setting targets and reaching targets … or it was about the ultimate consequence of failure. Bizarrely, some Home Office wag had thought it amusing to highlight that failure by signalling an impending termination with an aural blast of 3-2-1 from an aged game show, complete with virtual 3D fingers.

As a former politician, Megan had been a powerful voice in the drive to introduce the original CEU. It had been sold to a gullible public—packaged as a return to traditional values, a way of getting society back on the right path. If an individual could demonstrate usefulness, society wanted them, but those judged without value were out, with no chance of opting back in.

There were endless arguments as to what constituted usefulness, but everything shook itself out and into the right place in the end—once the Sliding Scale Tariff was imposed. Money almost guaranteed you a CEU. And power. That could get you a CEU. Get enough money and power and you could probably live forever.

As the dominant mindset surged on, read popular media, and further reinforced itself against the dangers of perceived compassion, so the mechanics of the original 1.0 CEU came to be viewed as outdated and not fit for purpose.

Government debate ensued, with the newly appointed Minister for Wellbeing declaring the 1.0, with its slot allocation for quick random death, to be 'completely opposed to entrepreneurship'. Ultimately, it was the suggestion that the 1.0 was encouraging an over dependence on the welfare state that rushed the 1.1 through Parliament. It was heralded as the government download everyone strives for, introduced to the public as progressive, enlightened, and fresh. Early fears of the download crashing at awkward moments or failing to complete—cue memories of an ill-fated NHS super computer—were smoothly ironed out. With a Health & Safety disclaimer and an Equality & Diversity mission statement, the 1.1 was rolled out with the claim of offering real choice and stating unequivocally that we were all equal.

'I don't really understand what you're looking for, Megan. Political analysts are secure in their conviction. The upgraded version has achieved spectacularly successful results in its core aims.' Carmen waved her bifocals around enthusiastically. 'You've achieved so much—a reduction in the undesirable elements of society, a re-energising of the need to succeed at all costs, and a reaffirmation that the individual is better than society.'

Carmen enveloped her friend in a bosomly hug and was shocked to find her cheek wet with Megan's tears. 'Oh, whatever's the matter, don't be scared.'

'It's not that, I'm too old to worry about that, but I think we've actually made things worse. Corruption seems to be an accepted part of life.'

Crime was an unforeseen but inevitable and ever-growing problem, especially with police forces replaced by a national CCTV system which was constantly crashing. How easy and irresistible for the strong to extend their already overinflated lives by mugging the weak for their little bit of an existence. A thriving online black market had sprung up. *'Do you need a bit of an extension?'* an affable chap would enquire as he emerged onto your computer screen. Or less affable, with a wolfish grin, *'Are you about to get terminated? Have you been offered an extension and been badly let down? Call Extensions 4u on...'*

'I sometimes think I chose the wrong side.' Megan's lips twisted as she forced a smile. 'Would it have been better to encourage people to come together and fight back, think about those around them a bit more and set their own targets for their future?'

Carmen leaned forward. 'But, Megan, these people don't know what's best for them. Better to be terminated than trapped, drawn into a false world of glamour and media misappropriation.'

No one could pinpoint with certainty the exact date of the Darcashinon emergence, but Carmen appreciated how effective the empire proved to be, although she despised herself for her involvement. A beautiful, shimmering chimera to keep the young and the poor happy and ensconced in a warm, deluded bath of endless breast implants, lip enhancements, and relationship traumas. Excitement lived through a camera lens because reality was oh-so-boring.

Carmen watched her friend with barely concealed anticipation.

Megan drew in a deep, shaky breath. 'I don't know. Maybe I am just getting old.'

Her friend chuckled. 'And foolish.'

Megan reached out a hand. 'I'd like to watch *Casualty*. Will you sit with me, Carmen?'

'Of course. You always did love that onscreen battle, didn't you? All that conflict and confrontation, just like being back in Parliament.'

Megan inserted her earphones and sat back, focussing on the screen. She hardly had time to register the shrill piercing noise before an expiration code sounded, and disembodied fingers flashed up: *3* then *2*, and then *1*.

A TABLE FOR ONE
By Julia Gale

I had been looking forward to having the first night in my new flat on my own, curled up in front of the television with a glass or two of my favourite tipple. My daughter Selena, however, had other ideas.

"How do you fancy going out tonight to celebrate, Mum?" she asked, just as we were unloading the last crate off the van.

"No thanks, I am far too tired. Perhaps another night?" I replied.

Once we had unpacked a couple of crates, I made a cup of tea for my daughter and me. It was getting late in the afternoon; Selena had to leave to collect her children from school.

"Are you sure you'll be ok, Mum?" Selena asked me just as she was leaving. I assured her I would be fine and that I would call her if there was a problem. However, I was not fine.

My husband had decided to leave me six months before, choosing after twenty-five years of un-blissful marriage to go and live with a woman much younger than myself; there was to be no reconciliation, not this time. Our youngest child left home a couple of months after my husband. That was when I made the important decision to sell our house and buy a flat in the next village, closer to where the children and their families lived.

After Selena left, I put the television on and started to do some further unpacking but quickly became bored – after all, I had been lifting and carrying boxes all day and my muscles ached. I poured myself a glass of wine and ran a bath to relax myself but could not.

After my bath, still feeling restless and more than a little hungry, I decided that maybe it would be a good idea to go out after all. It was late and I had not yet done any shopping. I picked up the telephone and tried to ring Selena but soon realised that it had not yet been connected. There was little charge left in my mobile but enough to make one call. I looked everywhere for the charger but could not find it.

Now it was getting dark and I found myself suddenly feeling very alone. Remembering that there was an old directory book by the phone, I picked it up and thumbed through it. Before long, I found what I was looking for: a nice sounding French bistro, which just happened to be very close to where I now lived. I rang them and they told me they could accommodate a late booking for one person that evening. So, feeling very excited, I managed to retrieve a reasonable-looking dress and an old pair of low-heeled shoes from one of the cases. I got myself dressed within minutes and before long was making my way downstairs and out of the door.

Feeling awkward and very self-conscious, I made my way down the road, hardly able to walk in my shoes. It had been, after all, some years since I had worn them last and they pinched. I became aware of people watching me: the only people in sight were a group of teenagers hanging around on the street corner; they appeared to find something amusing. I ignored them, took my shoes off and stuffed them into my bag, just in case the way I was walking happened to be the source of their amusement. I continued my journey barefoot.

At last, I arrived at the restaurant. I paused briefly in the doorway to look at the menu and to decide whether or not to venture in. I quickly made my mind up and entered the building.

"Bonjour Madame," the headwaiter greeted me cheerfully as I entered the restaurant. He was rather short, tubby, and in his mid-fifties; everything about him appeared to be false including his moustache and French accent. However, there was something familiar about him. He looked down disapprovingly at my bare feet and spoke to me with an arrogant tone, which I disliked instantly. "Ah yes, you are the late booking requesting a table for one, I believe?" Muttering, he led me to my table.

My table happened to be in the middle of the dining room. Looking around I saw table after table of happy couples, many of whom threw me a sympathetic glance or two. I decided to ignore them and picked up the menu. It was mainly written in French, of course, but as I just happen to be an ex- French teacher this was 'pas de problème' (not a problem), as they say in 'le langage de l'amour' (the language of love).

"Err, are you ready to order yet, Madame?" Suddenly I became aware of a young man standing beside me impatiently tapping his pen against the pages of a notebook; he had a bored, irritated look on his face.

He has obviously not served many people this evening, I thought to myself. I recognised him almost straight away; he was one of my former pupils. Jonny Brown was not one of my best students; however, I was secretly glad that he had managed to find himself a job. He did not appear to recognise me, therefore I decided to remain as anonymous as I could.

He took my order and returned to waiting on the other tables, glancing over his shoulder occasionally with a cheeky grin on his face. He knew from whom he had just taken the order!

I requested a bottle of Merlot to go with the French onion soup and beef bourguignon, and for dessert I ordered a light fluffy lemon mousse. As I sipped my wine, I began to feel relaxed and started to enjoy the surroundings. *Perhaps it's not so bad being on your own after all*, I thought.

It seemed like an eternity for the food to appear, the service was so slow; I finally received mine and tucked in gratefully.

A show began and three skinny, scantily clad young women appeared on the stage. They started singing and dancing badly. The audience appeared to enjoy it though, so I joined in with the clapping and cheering; it seemed as though I had no choice, being in the middle of the room.

Before long, I had company: a drunk. I tried to attract the attention of one of the waiters, but they were all far too busy. I decided that it was time to go home.

I left my table and let the drunk have the remains of my bottle of wine. All of a sudden I felt nauseous. The room started to spin, and I passed out.

I awoke lying in the middle of the restaurant with the headwaiter bending over me. "Are you ok?" he asked.

Jonny the waiter handed me a glass of water and I drank it slowly. When I had recovered sufficiently the headwaiter helped me up and sat me down on a chair. He told me his name was John and that Jonny the waiter was his son. I knew instantly where I had met him before: at the school.

Once I had fully recovered, John offered to walk me home as his shift had finished. I gratefully accepted, glad of the company.

John accompanied me into the flat; I was relieved and pleasantly surprised to find that the electricity had now been connected and it gave me the chance to offer him coffee for all his kindness. We conversed softly for some time whilst the night drew in and when he finally rose to leave, he wished me "bonne nuit" and gently slipped a piece of paper into my hand. Written on it were his address, telephone number and the words: "Contact me - only when you feel ready." This came as something of a surprise to me.

At first, my reaction was to put it in the bin, but a voice inside me told me to keep it. Maybe I would have the chance to discuss the events of the evening with Selena. Or, perhaps I was ready to start again after all.

One thing is certain. I went to bed that night a very happy woman.

SQUELCHFOOT
By Richie Stress

The handkerchiefs had not worked. That was the first thing he had noticed. Although the squelching of each step should have prepared him for what he was about to witness, the sight that greeted him as he removed the sodden sock from his right foot still managed to elicit a jab of shock.

The sock itself was unrecognisable from the one he had slipped onto his freshly showered and powdered foot that morning. The previous hue of virgin snow cotton replaced by a congealed, soggy mess of blood-soaked fibres.

After discarding the sock in the bin, Kevin washed the injury in the sink as best he could. He teetered and swayed as he worked, and anyone witnessing his efforts would have likened him to an overweight ballet dancer warming up at the bar.

With careful hands he wrapped some paper towels around the wound before loosening his shoelaces, as much as they would allow, then gently squeezed his toes into the shiny brown leather brogue.

He thought about making a dash, or rather a quick limp, towards the fire exit, when the toilet door opened, and an unfamiliar head stuck itself forcefully inside.

'Mr Troy? Ah there you are? Hello, my name is Mr. Grieves, and I will be your examiner for today. If you would just like to follow me and then show me to your car, we can begin the test lickety-split!'

*

Kevin had set his alarm for six-thirty that morning. The test was not scheduled to begin until nine, but he wanted to be prepared. Almost as soon as he had switched off his alarm, the telephone rang.

It was his driving instructor, Pete, calling to say that the car had a flat battery; that he would have to borrow a friend's car for Kevin to take his test in, and that Kevin should also make his own way to the test centre, if he would be so good, and that he apologised for any inconvenience caused.

Having calmly replaced the receiver, it took him well over two minutes to process and assimilate this information.

Rationally, with a few last-minute adjustments everything would still work out fine. In emotional terms, it felt like a strange carnivorous plant monster had emerged from the depths of Kevin's modest looking koi pond, wrapped itself around his entire body, then thrashed him around for a bit, before holding him upside down as it searched unceremoniously for a conveniently placed pool of quicksand in which to drown him.

He needed to think fast. No. Not only to think fast but also to act fast. This was not an easy thing to do when you are suddenly laden with two of your worst fears. The first of these was obviously the test itself. Luckily, he had prepared thoroughly and knew his Highway Code inside out and back to front. The second and more pressing fear was the very real possibility that he would be late or, even worse, miss the test altogether.

Ever since he was a child Kevin Troy had the almost morbid fear of not arriving on time. All through his school days, during his years at university and throughout his career in supermarket stock control, he had fostered an almost clinical dread of self-inflicted tardiness.

He was completely unaware of how this anxiety had come about. The truth being an event so hideously embarrassing that Kevin's mind had done a brilliant job of burying it down in the deepest recesses of his subconscious; somewhere so inaccessible that it would take a full fifteen years of future therapy sessions to uncover.

For the sake of full disclosure, the reader should be made aware that the incident in question involved a pop-up copy of *The Joy of Sex* borrowed from a relative's book shelf, an empty packet of cheese and onion crisps and a game of kiss chase with a girl known in the immediate locality as Randy Mandy. It is probably also worth noting that it was on this occasion that Kevin developed a lifelong aversion to cheese and onion crisps.

Scratching unnecessarily at his forearm now, Kevin could hear his heart beginning to thunder its way out of his lily-white chest. This familiar sound was drowned out by the noise of someone wheezing hysterically. Realising this someone was himself, he made a mental note—avoid a full-blown panic attack.

Another thought arrowed its way into consciousness. Even if he made the test, he was now obliged to use an alien vehicle that he had never seen before, let alone driven. He didn't even know what the make and model details were.

Surely there must be a rule somewhere dictating that a learner with a provisional licence was not allowed to take a virgin driving test in an unfamiliar car and, therefore, said learner driver was perfectly within their rights to demand a postponement of said test until such time that the car they had actually been learning to drive in, for the last thirty sessions, was again roadworthy.

Surely that was not too much to ask. Except, of course, he knew it was.

He curled his right toes into a fleshy ball; the digits pulled in so tight that the foot was numb within seconds.

He had breakfasted, showered, shaved and cleaned his teeth within half an hour. He figured that if he left by seven fifteen, he could get to the bus stop by seven thirty-five, and, provided the bus was prompt, the excruciatingly slow sixty-five-minute journey meant he would still make it in time.

Granted, he would not be in an ideal state emotionally, but by this stage it was the best he could hope for.

By the time he was ready to dash out of the house, his toes were throbbing, caused by the incessant rubbing, clenching and unclenching of his foot. Trimming his toenails was of course the one item of hygiene he had neglected during his meticulous preparation. Unfortunately, this meant that every time the five footy fingers on his right appendage flexed up and then down again, the jutting, overgrown nails would rub and, finally, cut into the neighbouring flesh. The skin was being flayed and began to bleed. Not that Kevin was immediately aware of this due to the effects of the initial adrenalin surge on his unsuspecting and very sensitive pain receptors.

He had somehow, throughout all of this, managed to maintain a precarious level of rational, functional calm. However, his body was now, for some reason, informing him of the worsening discomfort coming from his right lace-up.

Kevin ripped off his right shoe and sock, wincing in agony from the resulting sting. Studying the situation, he figured if he quickly cut the nails, he could at least stop the modest trickle of red leakage, literally stemming the tide as it were, before the situation got any worse.

He looked around madly for some scissors. The only ones that he was sure were in their designated location were his large pair of dressmaking scissors.

He wiped the blood from between his toes and tottered towards the kitchen. As long as he was careful, he could get the job done quickly and smartly and still make the bus with time to spare.

He sat on a stool and trimmed his baby toe—so far so good. Gaining confidence, he started on the ring toe—no problem. Moving on to the middle toe, he expertly sculpted it into a perfect semi-circle.

This was going to be easy. In his mind he started to celebrate. Against all the odds he had taken on life's curveball and was about to smash it out of the stadium for a home run.

No time for complacency though—two toes remaining: the most painful and cumbersome—the long toe and the undisputed king of toes, the hallux. The sound of a motorbike from outside caused him to jerk and almost pierce the end of his second little piggy.

Kevin tutted and began shaping the aptly named big toe. Having done half the job, he needed to change the angle of his foot to access the remaining area.

Reaching this part of the nail meant moving his foot from the edge of his stool where it was currently perched, and to then place it over his left knee. He dropped the scissors onto the floor and grabbed at his right foot with his left hand.

Greatly misjudging the swivel force needed, he somehow managed to twist his whole body causing the seat to slide backwards from under him. Instinctively, he released his right foot, attempting to stand up. Having narrowly avoided crashing to the floor he now felt a rather strange sensation coming from the sole of his newly pedicured foot.

Looking down in horror, he had somehow managed to stand on the sharp end of the scissors.

He sat on the floor and pulled the blades from the wound, assessing the damage. The cut was deep and now literally pumping blood out onto the pristine tiles below. He glanced at the clock—twelve minutes past seven.

Kevin sat on the bus trying as best he could to pretend that he was just a normal man on a normal day, taking a leisurely bus journey over to a driving test centre, where he would take his test. Such a man would then muse on whatever the outcome happened to be, take it in his stride and focus on the rest of his day. That is what an average and fairly balanced person would do.

For an unbalanced person, like Kevin had become, on his way to be judged by a stranger in a car he had never even seen, and with a wound worthy of a trip to A and E, the chances of the day ending on a positive note were, at this stage, questionable.

'Not taking yer test are ya mate?' Half an hour previously, the driver had chuckled to himself, as Kevin hobbled nobly onto the number 248 bus with his tattered copy of the Highway Code clearly on show.

He grunted noncommittally, not in the mood to engage with this man's cheery cockney banter. He hated being called 'mate'. Why did some men think it was OK to refer to another man as their mate when they had never met them before?

Worse than that, being addressed in such a manner was often a prelude to an act of aggression; 'Oi mate, do you have a problem with so and so?', or Kevin's favourite, 'Excuse me mate, you couldn't lend me a few quid for a cab, could ya?'—the interpretation being, 'if you *don't* give me some money, then there will be unpleasant consequences, and you don't want that do you?'

The bus trundled on slowly until it reached his stop, five minutes behind schedule. A man in a track suit with fluorescent yellow stripes alighted ahead of Kevin and strolled purposely in the direction of the British School of Motoring Test Centre, Eastbourne Branch.

Kevin had no clue as to who this man was, or even if he was heading in that direction to take a driving test. What he did know was that, outwardly at least, the man appeared annoyingly calm. There was even a hint of a self-satisfied confidence in the way he walked.

It was not fair, Kevin thought. Why did he not have the same confident strut? Why was he at this moment physically unable to walk with any dignity whatsoever? Why had this day of all days decided to conspire against him in such a way that he was now forced to shuffle along the pavement like a 200-year-old arthritic tortoise?

Mid-shuffle, a soot coloured Vauxhall Corsa S drew up beside him, but he ignored it.

'Hey Kev!' a voice called from the driver's window. Irritated, he glanced over. 'Look, I managed to get her started. Talk about cutting it fine, eh! Let me park up round back, and I'll meet you inside, ok.'

Before he had time to show any acknowledgement, he watched helplessly as Pete, his instructor, sped off towards the entrance of the test centre car park. He glanced down at his watch. Eight fifty-five a.m.

By the time he had reached the entrance, he was finding it increasingly difficult to walk. More alarmingly a faint squelching sound was beginning to issue from his shoe.

The receptionist smiled, pointed towards a row of seats and informed him that his examiner would be along shortly.

He sat down and winced. He knew there was a fair chance that he could stand the pain for the twenty minutes of the test. However, he also knew that there must be a fair amount of blood inside his shoe, and that any sight of claret would mean instant cancellation.

He could hear Pete chatting to someone outside, presumably a fellow instructor or maybe the stranger from the bus. Typical Pete, he could strike up a conversation with anyone. Kevin sighed before putting his Highway Code carefully into his inside jacket pocket then squelched stoically towards the gents.

TAKING A BATH
By Richard Miller

It had been a tiring day at the office and Carol wanted to arrive home as soon as possible, eat and then take a long, hot bath. She had been in the office for twelve hours, starting at 7.00am, and was now driving to her home in the countryside. A flat in a busy part of town and nearer work may have been more practical but Carol enjoyed the solitude of a house in the country. It allowed for time to relax after work, and long walks down country paths and through woods. The nearest neighbour lived about a mile away.

Having a high-pressure job, it was expected of her to work long hours nearly every day. Carol felt tired and stressed and this, combined with a painful divorce a couple of years ago, had caused her to lose a lot of weight. Thoughts of her ex-husband scared her as he had been a manipulative bully. Work had been a means of escape and at one stage the long working hours had kept her away from an awful home life. Convinced that her ex-husband wanted them to get back together and, worse, was stalking her, preyed on Carol's mind; without proof, however, that she was being stalked there were no grounds to go to the police.

Luckily, another man had appeared on the scene and a couple of weeks ago he had proposed to her. The new man in her life had put a spring in her step. Even though she still felt exhausted, she now had someone who listened and cared. As she drove home, Carol glanced at her engagement ring and saw it glisten every so often under the street lights.

Arriving home just after 9pm, Carol decided to make a sandwich to eat with a yoghurt and apple, washing them down with a glass of water. The thought of having to cook and then wait for nearly an hour to eat didn't appeal. Taking the yoghurt from the fridge, our recently engaged lady saw the opened bottle of white wine: a glass or several would make a nice accompaniment to her hot bath. Finishing off the bottle of wine would not be difficult.

Once the meal was finished, she ran the bath and added large amounts of bubble bath. In the background the soothing tones of a Joni Mitchell album emanated from the CD player. Placing the bottle and large glass on the surface next to the bath, Carol eased herself into the hot water and poured a hefty measure of sauvignon blanc. She brought the glass to her mouth. It appeared to have an unusual aroma but the temptation of wine and a hot bath conquered any thoughts of anything untoward.

Taking a large sip of the wine and thinking of her fiancé, she allowed the hot water and bubbles to pass over her. The clock on the wall of the bathroom showed 10pm. Half an hour in the bath and then bed. Carol pondered why she felt drowsy and sick: yes, it had been a tiring day, but there had been plenty of those in the past and one glass of wine had never had a bad effect before.

She awoke with a jolt and looked at the clock: two o'clock in the morning. The bath water was freezing. There was something else though: a throbbing in her left hand. Carol looked down. Her ring finger was missing and there was a pool of blood on the floor. Vomiting quickly followed. Then a man appeared in the doorway of the bathroom, holding a knife. "Hello Carol. Thought you could get rid of me?"

"What do you want, you bastard?"

"Now, now, no need to be rude. You know you miss me. I know we're divorced but it won't be too difficult to arrange a second marriage."

"What have you done to my finger? Where is my engagement ring?"

"Ah. I had hoped to remove the ring without cutting off your finger but that proved too difficult. I don't like that another man has given you something so nice. That's my prerogative. A good job I drugged your wine otherwise my job would have been more difficult. I knew you couldn't resist a glass or two when you come home. You're wondering how I knew that you were engaged? Well, I have my spies, and I wasn't happy when I found out."

"Why don't you bugger off, Steve. We're finished. I have a new man and he's a damn sight better than you'll ever be."

"That is not the answer you should be giving - or the one I wish to hear. Now you are going to listen to me while I do a little bit of explaining."

With that, Steve edged towards the bath. A scream rang out, but it would not be heard.

NEEDLESS NEEDLES
By Richie Stress

A knock: - my so-called friend; his Brother,
me and sister,
Crossing roads wrapped in a Winter Solstice.

♪ *trolling through the snow – on a load of worn out trays* ♪
Plastic sledges through dead hedges,
A gap in the trees – perfect!

Sister climbs on scared of
skidding sideways; stopping.
Left arse cheek, flayed it
feels like needles.

James' time,
No sense to slide,
Straight into the log

ambulance sleigh of broken legs.
'Have they kept him in?'
'Will he ever walk again?'

Running for the door in his pyjamas.

SLEIGH BELL BLUES
By Tony Ormerod

Good Evening and a Merry Christmas. My name is Dancer, I'm sure that many of you recognise the name. For many years now I have been part of an elite team that somehow, call it magic, manages to cover the entire planet in one night.

It's no picnic. I cannot fairly conceal that some of us just do not get on. Take Rudolph for a start. What a big-head! Okay, we might have taken the mickey when he first joined and, I suppose, that having a shiny red nose was no reason to mock, but I still think that the boss, who is in many ways kindness personified but, let's face it, past his best, was far too hasty in promoting a new boy who was simply too inexperienced.

Guiding the sleigh? The rest of us still laugh when we recall how we took a left instead of a right and ended up over China - not the biggest market for Christmas. In spite of that, Santa still thinks the sun shines out of Rudolph's, well, you know. In fairness, ever since then he has been stationed immediately behind me. Rudolph that is.

I like to think of myself as broad-minded as the next reindeer, but I am fed up with Rudolph's constant sniffing around my backside. Granted, our harnessing leaves little room for manoeuvre, but earlier tonight I'd had enough. I turned my head, as much as my diminished agility allowed, and spoke.

'Please kindly stop your sniffing back there,' I pleaded politely.

'You talking to me?' came back the haughty response.

'Yes you, Rudolph. I do wish you would keep your nose to yourself,' I said with all the authority a hundred years of loyal service has given me. 'It may be red, but hot it isn't!'

Young 'shiny nose' came back with: 'I've got a cold and I can't help it.'

'You've had the same cold for forty years?' said I. 'Pull the other one — it's got bells on.'

My colleagues laughed, their own bells tinkling as they shook.

So why don't you put in for a transfer? I hear you asking. Twice

I've tried, but no luck. There's a sweet thing called Vixen, she can't be a day over seventy, who I've always admired from afar. Although she's made the rear nearside position her own, I know that she would be happier with me stationed next to her, rather than that Teutonic bounder, Blixen.

'Nein danke, I am happy here viv my darlink Vixen,' Blixen protested, 'and I don't like Rudolph either.' I got no sympathy from Santa.

And where is our illustrious employer? Stuffing himself with mince pies and knocking back sherry in the warmth down below is where. Meanwhile we, the workers, are left fed up and shivering in the cold night air. Forget 'Goodwill to all Men.' How about a thought for us? I've a good mind to report him to the RSPCA! Not that I'm one to complain.

GUIDING STAR
By A.J.R. Kinchington

The fog plumed through the car window like huge ostrich feathers, partly obscuring vision and muffling any sound. Eerily, little drops of moisture hung above her in a threatening way. She noticed her cheeks were wet, as were the palms of her hands.

'Hmm, so much for planning.'

The sound of her voice startled her and she smiled ruefully at the thought of being late for her own wedding. She could almost hear the complaining drawl of her sister Babs, 'Just like Jenny, everything always at the last minute.' Babs had stayed close to their home in the Yorkshire Dales but Jenny had sought adventure and romance. The opportunity arose when she was offered a teaching post in London.

Jenny had never considered marriage, let alone to Nathan. They had been introduced by a friend and had been dating for a year. Her friends called Nathan a 'nice guy' and 'a good catch' and although she agreed with them, she had hoped to walk on cloud nine not walk down the aisle. It was his promotion to the New York office that heralded his proposal and his excitement swept her along. This evening was to be a quiet family wedding and they were scheduled to fly to New York in the morning, and yet…

The last few days had been hectic as she packed up her belongings in the flat. A virus had caused the school to close and although she felt unwell, she dismissed her high temperature and sickness as pre-wedding nerves.

Being alone did not usually bother Jenny but being swallowed up by this fog on the moors unnerved her. She tried her mobile but it was unresponsive. She leaned over the steering wheel and wound up the window. The world outside felt hostile and her neck and head were aching.

Patting the pale lace skirt of her dress, she glanced down at the black trainers housing her cold and restless feet. 'Cold feet (the metaphor not lost on her), restless and utterly lost,' she murmured, shivering.

Ahead of her she saw what she thought was a car's headlight, but it was brighter than anything she had seen before. It came from above. Silver strands puncturing the grey veil of the stratus cloud and pooling in astral splendour.

She wondered if she was hallucinating; nevertheless, she drove towards it.

Later, she would recall that it was the last thing she remembered doing.

*

Steve and his three-year-old daughter, Senga, were outside in the cold night air. Steve felt his daughter's arms round his neck and her soft, freshly shampooed hair against his face. His emotions were near the surface and he squeezed her hard. She had pleaded with him to go into the garden to search the sky for that one special star. He thought the fog would obscure it but could not deny he needed to see it too.

'Where are you, where are you?' Senga sang out loud, waving her arms. Steve joined in, their voices offered up to the skies. Threads of moonlight penetrated the soft duvet of fog and for the waiting audience below, the night star performed as only it could. Rewarded, the pair went indoors where Steve's mother, Agnes, had warm drinks waiting for them and an embrace for her son. Later, she would read Senga's favourite bedtime story. The Christmas story had taken on significant meaning since Senga pronounced Bethlehem as Bethanyhem.

Steve liked his forty-minute drive to work. His route took him up over the moors, then down to the small town of Ingleton. It was where he had first seen Beth, her dark hair hidden beneath her police cap, but shaken down round her shoulders, well, that was something else. Her eyes had been dark, darker when aroused. Her death two years ago made him question everything except his love for Senga. Mummy's special star was something they shared.

The isolation of these moors mirrored his mood and brought with it a prevailing sense of feeling lost.

His reverie was broken by the sight of the blue car sitting at an odd angle in the layby. It sat in a circle of light in the slowly lifting fog. He flicked his car lights to full beam and drew up alongside. She lay motionless across the front seats, her hair hiding her face.

'Miss, can you hear me? I'm Steve, a police officer.'

She half opened her eyes. 'Jenny. I'm lost.' She tried to sit up but failed.

'Don't worry, help is coming.'

In the twenty minutes it took for the ambulance to arrive he had covered her in a blanket and radioed her car registration to the police station.

The hospital at midnight was quiet. Steve parked his patrol car and went to enquire how Jenny was. Her sister Babs was outside the ward.

'Steve Bailey, remember me? Barbara – Babs – Gilchrist. We were in the same class – Ingleton High.'

'I thought the name was familiar but couldn't place Jenny.'

'She was in a class two years below us.'

At that moment a nurse came out of a side ward. 'Miss Gilchrist is comfortable. The virus has exhausted her. She will be in overnight. You can see her for a few moments.'

Steve removed his cap and noiselessly entered the ward.

Jenny was bathed in soft night light, her long blond tresses framing her pale and delicate face.

He was shaken at the impact she had on him. He felt heady, as if he had been drinking a love potion.

Jenny was between wakefulness and sleep. She saw him standing at the foot of her bed, his six-foot frame dressed in a dark uniform. Stray black curls rested on his forehead, a shy, slow smile playing on his generous mouth. She closed her eyes, breathed out a long sigh and drifted away on a cloud that resembled the number nine.

Babs was waiting for him. 'Steve, we must all get together again when Jenny comes home. Thank goodness you found her in time.'

Steve nodded, timing was everything. He walked out into the cold dawn morning and raised his cap to the universe and one star in particular.

A NEW BEGINNING
By Julia Gale

Sheila's day should have begun exactly the same way as it had for more than thirty years. Ever since she had started her teaching career, she would get up at exactly 5.30 a.m., have breakfast and walk her two Irish setters, Chloe and Cleo. She would then prepare a simple meal for later, get into the car and drive to the school where she was the Head Teacher.

But today was going to be different. Shelia had dreaded this day for a long time. Not only because it happened to be her 61st birthday, but also because it was her final day at work. Sheila had never relished the idea of retiring. Teaching had been her life ever since she first came to England from Ireland all those years ago.

She had just returned home after walking the dogs and was about to get ready to leave for work when she noticed that there was a message on the answering machine.

Who could be ringing me at this early hour? She wondered as she pressed the play button. Sheila instantly recognised the voice on the recording. It was Jayne Thompson, her secretary of many years.

'Hello Sheila, I do hope that I'm not too late and you are not already making your way to school. Mr Palgrave has asked that you don't come in too early this morning as the staff and children are planning a surprise for you.'

Sheila disliked surprises but reluctantly agreed to Mr Palgrave's unusual request. He was her deputy Head Teacher and the most likely candidate to take over the Headship from her after she left. *I hope he manages to keep the children under control, they're an unruly bunch at the best of times!* Sheila thought jokingly.

She had known from the start that Mr Palgrave would be a worthy successor, even though he was still in his early thirties. He was an experienced teacher, strict but popular with both staff and children. Sheila had, however, always run the school with the discipline and order she herself had been taught to uphold. She was aware that some of the decisions she had made during her time as Head Teacher had not always made her popular with the staff, pupils or their parents. Not that it had unduly bothered Sheila as she never had much time for socialising or the need for friends anyways.

'I hope they're not planning a party for me. They should know that I hate parties,' Sheila said out loud as she stood in front of the mirror combing her long, greying hair. Her hair had been ginger in her youth. Her father had always told her that a woman's hair is her crown and forbade her mother, Sheila, and her sisters, to have their hair cut or changed.

Sheila had always taken pride in her appearance, making sure her hair was always tied into a firm bun and her make-up flawless. Today was not going to be any exception.

Having time to spare was a new experience to Sheila and it made her quite uncomfortable. She looked around her house trying to find something to occupy herself with but found nothing. Her housekeeper, Mrs Johnson, came twice a week and always left the house spotless. Resigned, Sheila went into the kitchen and prepared a snack and a cup of tea. She sat down, put some relaxing music on and let her mind drift, reflecting on her life so far.

Sheila had grown up in Belfast during the sixties and the youngest of five children. The family had lived in a tiny terraced house in the Shank Hill area. It was a closely-knit community even at the height of the religious troubles of the time. Everyone knew Sheila's family, especially since her father was a lay minister at the local protestant church and had a lot of powerful friends, including a few who were also involved in local politics. This did not always make him popular within the community. It was often dangerous for Sheila and her siblings to venture out, especially when there was rioting outside their house. It was during those times that the children were unable to get to school.

Sheila had always been a shy, studious child who enjoyed her own company. She had never liked school, despite her desire to become a teacher herself one day. She had often felt different from the other children.

Her parents, Patrick and Julie, were strict and almost Victorian when it came to raising their five children. Patrick was a large man with ginger hair, moustache, beard and a fiery temper to match his red hair. Her mother, Julie, was the complete opposite to her husband, small and soft-spoken. They were, however, both deeply religious. Patrick rarely spared the rod if a member of the family upset him. Having once worked at the shipyard, a job he had enjoyed, Patrick had always brought home a good income - until one day, whilst climbing a ladder at work carrying paint pots in both hands, he lost his footing and fell. The fall left him with severe head injuries. He spent a long time in hospital and when he was sufficiently recovered, he returned home. The accident had not only had an impact on Patrick's life, but also on his whole family. His now continuous mood swings made him violent and unfit to work. Julie was forced to leave her teaching job to look after him. From then on money was always tight. The eldest children had to find jobs doing whatever they could and life was never the same again.

Her father's often violent mood swings had frightened Sheila. She had seen the effect they had on her mother and found life at home becoming increasingly difficult. No longer could she speak to her mother about things as she had done in the past, she was always too busy. Her brothers and sisters were now leading their own lives with families of their own, so no longer had time for her 'wee Sheila', or so it seemed to her.

When her exams finally finished, she persuaded her parents to let her go and find casual work for a year just over the border in Eire, promising them that she would return the following year to do teacher training at university. Her parents reluctantly agreed to let her go. She found being on her own hard at first, after all she had come from a large family. But before long she met Peter. Peter was tall and thin and had the greenest eyes Sheila had seen in her life. He was soft spoken and gentle, also a Catholic and a hippy. Sheila knew her parents would never agree to her seeing him, but this only made him even more attractive to Sheila and before long they had fallen in love.

Peter had a very persuasive nature and soon Sheila found herself dying her hair and wearing long flowing dresses and skirts just to please him. He made her feel special. Peter often spoke to Sheila about a hippy commune close to his hometown and about his desire to one day become a part of it with her if that was what she wanted. Sheila did not take too much time to make her decision, she had become bored with fruit picking. Within a week they had packed up to start a new adventure together.

At first Sheila revelled in the freedom the commune provided, and she quickly made new friends. However, it was not long until the novelty of living a life of peace, love and psychedelic hazes lost its appeal. Shelia had discovered quite soon after they had moved in that she was pregnant with Peter's baby. He was angry and indignant at the news. He lost interest in her and in no time found a new girlfriend.

They left after a disagreement with the commune leader leaving Sheila alone, although her new friends offered her their support. But she soon realised that community life was no place to bring up a child. There was only one thing she could do and that was to return home and face the consequences.

When Sheila told her parents her news their reaction was as she expected. Her father was furious. He took off his belt and hit Sheila with it until she was sore. Patrick vowed to kill Peter should he return, looking for Sheila.

Her mother insisted that she stayed confined at home for the rest of her pregnancy. Then after the baby was born Sheila was to have it adopted. Miserable, Sheila agreed with her parents' decision. For the next few months Sheila barely left the room she used to share with her three sisters. Memories of happier times flooded her mind but somehow, they seemed to make things worse.

The time came for the baby to be born; it was a girl. Sheila named her Isla.

Sheila had hoped that her parents would warm to idea of a grandchild once the baby had been born and that she would be allowed to keep her, but it just made them even colder towards her and Isla. Sheila became worried for both the safety of her baby and herself. Being at home was no place for her to bring up a child either. Besides, her father's condition had worsened in the time she had been away and her mother had enough to cope with. Within a fortnight, social services had come to take Isla to be adopted by 'a nice couple in England'. That was all they could tell Sheila as she signed her daughter away to a life of uncertainty.

Heartbroken, Sheila stayed in her room with the few items she had left to remind her of Isla. She was overcome with feelings of grief, anger, hurt. She refused food and slept little.

When she did try to venture out, she was aware of people looking at her, staring and sniggering - it was a close-knit community and news spread quickly.

Sheila could only see one way out of her situation and that was to leave Ireland behind for England, to find her baby and perhaps do the teacher training that she so eagerly desired. She packed a bag, left her mother a note and made her way to the ferry terminal to catch the midnight ferry bound for Liverpool.

Sheila was awoken by the sound of her phone ringing. Sleepily she answered it, again, she heard her secretary's voice.

'Sheila, where are you? I know Mr. Palgrave asked you to come in later, but this is a little ridiculous don't you think?'

'Why, what time is it?' Sheila enquired.

'It is two-thirty, school is almost closing and the children are waiting for you!'

Sheila told her secretary that she would be there straight away. Hastily, Sheila got herself ready and drove to the school.

What a sight greeted her when she arrived! Balloons and decorations filled the hall and all the children and staff from her many years of teaching had gathered to wish her well. A small party followed, but Sheila didn't mind this time.

Sheila left the school that evening a happy woman. She filled her car with all the cards, presents and balloons.

So, what's going to happen now? She wondered, as she drove away. One thing was certain, she had decided that joining the WI, making strawberry jam and knitting for children in Africa was really not for her.

As she arrived home, she went to the bureau and pulled out an old letter, still unopened. Her mother had written to her after her father passed away. It contained an address, the address of Isla's adoptive parents. Her mother had known where her baby was all these years.

Sheila knew then what she wanted to do with her retirement. Perhaps there was still time to be able to find Isla and make up for the lost years.

It would truly be a new beginning.

MUD PIE
By Richie Stress

We stick by ourselves with little,
to gain war wounds: fresh afraid.
Confused in fragrances,
listing mustard and rose wine.

From deep down:
a notion of pity that lunges around
a burden, as heavy as planets.
But we are not gods.

Flinching in dreams
like broken hyenas.
'Let us fly, let us die,
let us eat mud pie.'

For liberty of choice and causes,
signs that men shall rise,
but never be rewarded. Until
the kick inside.

LONG OVERDUE
By Richard Miller

I have lost count of the books I have at home and am running out of space to store them. Every so often I have to buy more cases to house them. But owning so many books doesn't stop me from buying more. I should be banned from visiting book shops. And it's not only shops I visit; libraries are also a wonderful place to go - but they also have a dark side.

How can a library have a dark side? Well, let me explain. My local library opens at 9.30am and closes at 5pm each day from Monday to Saturday. On three of my last four visits I have turned up at 4.50pm – my own fault, I am so disorganised – expecting to hand in books and borrow some more. I was able to borrow on one of the occasions, but only as one of the staff had to work late. Turning up at ten minutes to closing time on the next two occasions I was greeted with the pronouncement: "You can return books but not take any away. If you wish to borrow any, come back tomorrow."

As I started to moan, the librarian stared at me and I had to accept being told off.

On the fourth occasion I turned up just as the library was closing. "Not you again. Don't you have a watch? You'll have to come back tomorrow. We're closed and you'll have to pay the fine for late returns."

Today, I was determined to arrive at the library long before 5pm so I would have ample time to return books and choose new ones to read. But as Rabbie Burns wrote: '*The best laid schemes o' mice an' men*....' Things went wrong from the time I awoke. The washing machine flooded the kitchen; my car wouldn't start, and I couldn't find one of the books to return so – you've guessed it – I didn't arrive at the library until 4.45pm. After returning the books I headed to the horror and crime sections; given what would happen later this was most appropriate. Knowing which stories I wished to borrow I took them from the shelves and quickly headed towards the desk. The clock struck five as I placed the books on the desk and handed over my card to the librarian, who said, in a way indicating that I was being told off: "You can borrow the books even though you're late again but on one condition. You'll have to help out one of our staff in sorting out some books. I hope you've eaten. It could be a late night."

Staring at the desk, I mumbled: "I can't. I'm meeting someone for a meal. I'll come back tomorrow to borrow these."

Staring coldly at me, the employee uttered sinisterly: "If you don't help us, you'll be banned from this library."

I thought: banned from a library? That would be like cutting off a hand or having my eyes gouged out! I struggled for words to argue my case, but none came.

"Excellent," the librarian declared. "Now that's settled, my colleague will show you what's required."

At that moment, a large man appeared from the office behind the desk. He looked as if he could go fifteen rounds with Mike Tyson. Beckoning me to follow, he led me towards one of the storerooms and gave me my instructions. Before my boss for the night left me to work elsewhere, he told me he would return in two hours to check up on me.

As I settled down to do what was required, I pondered the reason: all because I was late. It seemed harsh. The threat of being banned from the library was depressing and hung over me like a great weight.

The storeroom I was in had a great number of tomes about horror and crime: two of my favourite genres. Horror stories by King, Herbert, Hutson and crime novels from the pens of Rendell, Hill and Camilleri: all fine experts in their craft. Engrossed in my job, I didn't notice that the lights in the library had been switched off and I was alone in the building. It was only when I looked at my watch I saw that I had been working for three hours; no one had come to check up on me.

Leaving the storeroom, I groped around in the dark in the hope of finding a light switch. I called out but received no response. After my eyes adjusted I found my way to the front door, but it was locked. Not having a mobile, I staggered to the desk to use the phones there: neither worked. It was then I heard sounds coming from the storeroom.

On entering the room I noticed about twenty-five novels on the floor. Some had been put on the floor by me - but not as many as there were now. As I bent down to pick up one of the books the pages started to turn. Given that there were no windows or air-conditioning I was at a loss as to what was causing the leaves to move. What happened next, had me rooted to the spot and I was left shaking and sweating profusely.

From the pages of the works on the floor appeared characters. All created by that genius, Stephen King, some were instantly recognisable: the evil clown Pennywise from IT and the rabid Cujo from the tale of the same name. I guessed at other characters as they appeared: George Stark, the wicked twin of the gentle Thad Beaumont in The Dark Half; The Dark Man, with power to manipulate and deceive, from my favourite King epic, The Stand; and even the possessed car, Christine.

From the crime novels rose perpetrators and culprits who joined the horror characters in forming a circle, as if they were to participate in an ancient rite, and spoke, barked or made engine noises. The voices were not how I imagined the characters would speak. One of the characters looked at me, pointed and moved towards me. Dread engulfed me. I wondered what they would do to me: would I be tortured? They grabbed hold of me and started to drag me towards one of the books, The Stand. I tried to flee from their clutches but was too weak with fear to fight. My assailants were pushing me into the horror classic. I love the book but didn't want to be part of it. The question was: how on earth could I, a living being, become part of a book? I knew the expression 'Lost in a good book', but this was ridiculous.

As I was being pushed into the book other characters appeared from the pages. These were the good people: Inspectors Montalbano, Wexford, Dalziel and Dalgleish from the pens of Camilleri, Rendell, Hill and James respectively; the seven children from It, who took on and defeated Pennywise; and Stu Redmond, Larry Underwood and Fran Goldsmith, who went to battle with the Dark Man.

What happened next was a battle for my body and soul as I was pulled one way and the other, the evil ones trying to take me into the book and the good folks trying to keep me in my world. Punches and kicks were thrown; curses were uttered and exclamations of revenge proclaimed. I was sure I would be torn to pieces. I heard someone with a heavy Italian accent shouting: "He's not of the book world, leave him be." Montalbano, I presume, as he is the only Italian detective I know.

I felt my legs go further into the novel. The good guys were losing the battle. I didn't want to be part of a book. I wanted to read books. Other characters from both sides had now joined the fray. It appeared that every character from every book which had ever been written was now in the storeroom. I imagined Miss Haversham with an axe trying to chop off the heads of my enemies.

"For god's sake," I shouted, "let me stay."

I can't recall much of what happened next. I must have been knocked unconscious. Waking up in the main part of the library, I looked up to see the librarian, who now looked like he *had* gone fifteen rounds with Mike Tyson. His smile indicated he knew what had happened and that I had been lucky. In his hand was a large mirror, which he held to my face. I saw that I was covered with stamps. Only two words, but my face was covered with them... Long Overdue.

Never again would I be late taking books back to a library.

AN OLD PENNY
by Glynne Covell

The hand bell clanged loudly in the school playground, heralding a tumultuous noise of desks slamming shut, chairs grinding on stone floors and yells of joy as the boys and girls ran from their classroom into fresh air and freedom.

Tom and Armand caught sight of one another in the yard and waving furiously, they turned and fled in the same direction from the school grounds, out into the street and towards the river.

'Let's do the bridge first,' cried Armand. 'I'll race yer!'

Passing by the noisy wharves and dockers, busy with their loads, the lads ran full speed, knocking into angry pedestrians and nearly falling over a stray dog.

'Watch it you damn hooligans,' yelled a city gent, dressed in suit and cap. 'You should know better at your age!' He raised his hand to give them a clout.

Both the boys were ten years old and lived in the same street in Rotherhithe, born into families of dockers. There was a strong community spirit amongst these river people; they looked out for one another, generous and warm-hearted despite having very little in their lives. Life was tough, accommodation cramped for the generally large families — a time of make do and mend. Children were left to fend for themselves, but they knew no different and for them, life was for living.

It was over a year since the general strike of 1926, and the docks were resuming their importance on the Thames. Many workers were downcast and low-spirited with the struggle to provide for their families, but the children, born and raised around the sights and smells of the river and the magnificent Tower Bridge, delighted in their setting. This was life. Some days were spent travelling to the other side of the river, a most daring and dangerous feat. They would hold onto the back of a horse-drawn carriage for grim death as the horses pulled the load through the Rotherhithe Tunnel. They emerged on the other side, shaken but victorious, and considered themselves 'abroad'.

Their clothes were testament to the hard life experienced by many Londoners. Short flannel trousers worn flat by wear and held up by braces; more often than not hand-me-downs from older members of the family. Shirts and jumpers, darned and mended again and again, and shoes badly scuffed and sporting holes in the soles. Who cared? Certainly the young lads didn't.

Today, however, Tom and Armand were collecting cigarette cards discarded by smokers as they dropped their empty packets crossing to and from the City. Both lads had a great collection of these colourful cards and a favourite pastime was to swap duplicates in the playground.

'This rain is getting heavy,' said Tom. 'Let's go down to the Mayflower and see if we can earn a penny or two.'

'Yeah right, we might as well get wet in the river,' answered Armand.

They turned abruptly, nearly knocking over an old lady carrying her pitcher of ale from the pub.

'Get out of it you dirty scallywags! Nearly lost me drink! Watch where you're going.'

Ignoring her cries, they ran on in the pouring rain through Rotherhithe, passing the cold stores of Jamaica Road, jumping over crates and ropes of the dockers and lightermen. The smells of the docks hung heavy around them. A heady mix of tobacco, spices and fruit blended with the odour of horses and sweat from the workers. The boys continued past St Mary's Church, along the cobbled road made slippery with the rain to the old fifteenth-century Mayflower Inn. By the side of the inn there was a narrow alleyway with steps that led down to the Thames. Here, they joined another lad, Nelson, already undressed and about to enter the water. This was the time when help was always appreciated to get the ferry boats to the shore from their mooring, ready for the watermen to transfer any passengers from one side of the river to the other. There was a penny to be made for the boys and it saved the waterman getting wet.

Scrambling out of their clothes, they jumped into the cold, filthy, brown water ignoring the stench from the murky depths. This was where they had learned to swim, emerging covered in grease and oil, gradually learning a few strokes to survive. Many a beating had they endured on arriving home looking like oil slicks. Occasionally, one of them caught an eel in his trouser leg, which had escaped from the cages underneath the large boats that were transporting from Holland. It was a bonus to take an eel home for tea as well as a penny or two. There had been a few tragedies some years ago when young lads had swallowed poisonous substances from the river. Factories were accused of discharging their waste straight into the water but nothing deterred the lads; this was their playground.

*

Seventy-nine years on, Tom stood on the balcony at the back of the Mayflower, sipping his pint of brown ale. Looking down on the river, it seemed like only yesterday that he and Armand had learned to swim in that very water.

That dreadful day, so many years ago, weighed heavily on Tom's shoulders. He wiped a tear from his eye as more memories flooded back. Armand, in his eagerness to release the tethered boat from the mooring, had dived down and disappeared. A wrong move. His left foot had become entangled with the ropes and he was trapped beneath the surface of the river. Tom and Nelson had done what they could trying to release their friend, but to no avail. Bert the waterman had raised the alarm, but poor Armand had gone by the time help had arrived. Another fatality claimed by the river. The verdict had been drowning by misadventure, and the family never got over their loss. Tom, too, had never really recovered from that tragic day, and standing here with events of that time playing out in his mind were like shards of glass torturously cutting into his heart and soul. He had carried the burden of the loss of his dear friend all these years.

Tom felt in his pocket for the old Victorian penny that he always kept, now worn smooth and thin by constant handling. It gave him great comfort having this link to bygone days, consoling his ageing body and weary mind. Now and again he came here and let himself be immersed in the memories, the sounds and smells of that time long ago; the fateful day that had haunted him all his life through the years of growing up, serving in the war, his career in the police and his family life.

'Are you ready now Dad?' Armand said as he put a comforting arm around Tom's shoulders. 'Time to get you back home for tea.'

'Yes son, I'm done,' answered Tom, taking one more glance at the Thames, the river of so many memories, his hand still clutching the old penny.

A PARTICULAR MAN
By Jan Brown

Bennett Morley was a particular man. He sat very still at the huge oak dressing table and plucked brutally at one or two odd nose hairs which had the temerity to peep out. His fine, arched eyebrows and smooth skin came courtesy of GravitasMan in the Strand, but nose hair Bennett dealt with privately. Bennett didn't really have friends but would tell his acquaintances: 'The need for self-control is the one thing I learnt from my parents.'

Bennett had been a particular child too. His mother, Frances, all fluffy blonde hair and fluttering fingers, had often explained away his lack of emotion to neighbours.

'He's very particular, my Bennett. He knows what he likes.'

In the long and dark winter nights, the seven-year-old Bennett had often thought of his mother eulogising his likes and dislikes, his thick lustrous lashes glistening with tears long after silence had descended on the school, but he had quickly learnt the folly of emotion.

The impassive, clear blue eyes of the now 35-year-old Bennett stared back at him, and he nodded, acknowledging himself in the full-length mirror. Grey pinstripe perfection. He had been planning this visit for a long time, going back to his old school, dreaming of the day he could walk down the long, echoey corridors without fear. Bennett decided he would still avoid the north staircase; even after all these years, Piggy Wilkins was not easily forgotten.

Bennett sat in the silver Jaguar for ages after parking, stroking the cool leather and staring at his reflection in the driver's mirror. He pictured his aged, long-departed father making the same journey.

'Don't leave me here, Father, please.' Even with churning insides, the young Bennett had retained his manners.

'Nonsense, Bennett, my boy. Mabbotscombe Prep will make a man of you.' His father awkwardly ruffled Bennett's soft gentle curls one last time and, removing himself from his son's grasp, handed him a sturdy leather suitcase.

'We've talked about this. Your Mother has thoroughly researched everything; this is the best place for your specific needs.'

Bennett brushed imaginary specks from his immaculate suit, straightened his tie and marched through the imposing wooden double doors. The school's common room, now prosaically named "The Residents Lounge" didn't look that different to how he remembered it, but the occupants were from another era. He couldn't find her at first; they all looked the same, their old, watery cloudy eyes peering at him hopefully.

There she was. Her hair was still blonde, but he could now see the pate flashing obscenely through the fluff. Her fingers were trembling rather than waving.

'Hello Mother.' Bennett smoothed his hand across his trim, unresisting hair and stood looking down, before finally bending towards her and aiming his right cheek vaguely in her general direction.

'How have you been, Mother? Best not get too close. You know what these places are like for spreading germs.'

Endeavouring to keep his focus fixed on an over-sized vase of dried flowers near the window, he heard a voice.

'Well, well, well, if it isn't Spindles Bennett visiting his delightful aged parent.'

Piggy Wilkins appeared from behind the huge wicker elephant that took up much of the room, his eyes scrunched up with glee.

'I thought it might be you when I saw the next of kin details.'

As Piggy flicked the tip of his tongue in and out with obvious enjoyment, Bennett struggled to breathe, buried memories resurfacing.

'How you doing, Spindles? Fallen down any staircases lately?'

Look down, don't look at him.

'Wh...what are you doing here?' Bennett mumbled.

Piggy leaned in close to Bennett and waved an ID badge at him.

'I like taking care of the old folk, and they...' he paused and caressed Frances' neck, firmly, 'very much like taking care of me.'

A POINT OF VIEW
By C.G. Harris

Dad was brilliant today. When my friends (no girls!) arrived for my 8th birthday party, he said hello to all of them and smiled a lot, and then took their coats upstairs to hang up; when he got back he did some magic tricks for us.

Most of us pretended not to notice when he put that card in his pocket. Charlie Higgs was all for shouting it out loud until I gave him a Chinese burn and got Porky Allen to sit on him. Dad says it's not politically correct – whatever that is – to call someone a name like that. Of course, Porky doesn't know we call him that; we're not stupid – he'd kill us!

Mum brought the food in and we followed Porky's lead and dug into the cakes. The sandwiches were left untouched; I could see Mum looking a bit glum, so I nibbled at a cheese sandwich until she wasn't looking, then shoved it behind the sofa.

We went into the garden where Dad had organised some games, but the best bit was when Dad tried to show how good he was at football. He was crap. We laughed our heads off! But he did do a fantastic header from a cross by Charlie that went straight past Porky who was in goal – which takes a lot of skill as Porky fills most of it up.

I think Dad enjoyed the party even more than I did!

*

Harold was feeling nervous. The bell rang; and when he opened the door a gang of kids swept in – he couldn't see how many, but they damn near knocked him over. While they rushed past him and threw their coats at him, he made himself smile. He took the coats upstairs and stood there uncertainly; then he thought, *sod it,* and flung the coats on the bed.

He was apprehensive about the little magic display that he had been working on, but after the event he was confident that it had gone well (so easy to fool these kids!). He had an uneasy suspicion that the little bugger (what was his name – Charlie?) had spotted something, but he felt that he had got away with it.

The food went down well, at least the cakes did; he knew they wouldn't eat the sandwiches, even the chubby lad didn't want them!

They were sods in the garden. It was a waste of time organising games; all they wanted to do was play football. Harold didn't mind that too much, he thought he could show them a thing or two, and things were going fine until that bloody Charlie smashed the ball into his face. He had a notion it was deliberate – Christ it hurt! He was still rubbing his face when the lot of them buggered off. Thank God!

This story was first published October 2017 in 'Light and Dark: 21 Short Stories' by C.G. Harris, which was shortlisted for the Georgina Hawtrey-Woore Award 2018 for Independent Authors. Book available on Amazon.

HERMES
By Richie Stress

At first glance the land appeared barren. Dirty grass wasteland trailed off in every direction, framed on all sides by hard grey mountains. The air bore the scent of emptiness and fear and a bitter wind blew with the blind certainty of warning.

In an instant she knew she was an intruder; anxiety screamed at her to turn back now or else. Or else what? Perhaps death? She walked on, unsure of what she was doing here.

She hadn't gone far when she stumbled onto a kind of broken pathway stretching out to her left. It was probably a good idea to find out where it led.

As she turned along the track, she spied something up ahead. Several hundred metres from where she stood: a movement. Her cold skin felt the pricking of a thousand glowing needles and she started to shiver, but managed to control her breathing. Come on, Veronica. The last thing she needed out here in the Canadian Rockies was a bloody asthma attack.

She fumbled inside her satchel for her pump and took a generous puff. As she regained control of her senses, squinting into the grey-green wilderness, she made out a shape. It was an animal of some kind, the size of a big dog, she thought; its outline was indistinct against the gloom. Could it be the sort of beast one read about in the local paper; a monster who roamed the land hunting its quarry? It approached her, breaking into a clumsy trot.

Veronica laughed and sighed with relief, as what was now clearly a bighorn sheep drew level. It looked lost and pathetic, its eyes touched with disappointment; perhaps it had hoped to find a fellow member of the flock to lead it safely back to its kin. It had probably not expected a middle-aged woman indulging in some mad-arse quest for God knew what.

'Shoo! Go away! I'm just as lost as you are.' Veronica waved her hands at it. The sheep ignored her, stopping close by and starting to graze on the sparse foliage.

Gazing up at the darkening sky, she saw that, soon, all of nature would be obscured in its relentless embrace. It would be complete, she realised, no tame, luminescent city blackness, but the blindness of biblical ferocity.

She walked on. Not because she knew where she was heading but because it was preferable to the alternative—waiting, and for who knew how long.

Bighorn trotted happily by her side. It had got over its initial regret and seemed quite content to be led somewhere, anywhere, by anyone.

The broken trail continued westwards, towards another range of rocky hills. It was obvious that sheep could survive out here in the middle of nowhere and if that were true then she determined that she could too.

Heading north again, they had been travelling for roughly a mile when Veronica tripped and fell awkwardly. Looking down she found she had stumbled on something buried in the earth. A closer inspection revealed a slim shaft; she leaned over and yanked it clear. As it came free it made a peculiar rattling noise.

It was a vicious hunting knife with a serrated blade. She shuddered at the thought of someone here in the wilderness carrying such a thing, but then reasoned that it made sense, that in fact this would be perfect territory for survival training. The rattle appeared to be coming from inside the bone handle, although the handle itself seemed solid enough.

Well, at least now she could defend herself from whatever nasties crossed her path. She stood with difficulty and winced; pain shot through her right ankle.

Not wanting to consider the consequences of an injury she limped onwards, placing the knife in her trusty leather satchel as she hurried after her roaming companion. In her haste she fell again, hard, sending new shocks through her ankle and striking her knee sharply on a lump of rock.

Panic now set in. The throbbing in her knee threatened to overwhelm her, and her ankle had swollen up alarmingly. She pushed herself up to sitting, drawing strength from the rough earth, and watched her companion grazing unconcernedly in the distance. Summoning a weak voice, she called after it and to her surprise it turned obediently and wandered back.

Several minutes passed. Her choices now were limited to say the least. How to survive out here until help came; if it came? Maybe she could kill the sheep with her new knife; then she could eat it raw, or climb inside its innards to keep warm like that guy from Star Wars.

The sheep had its back to her. She slid the blade from her bag, but as she raised it to strike the rattling sound alerted the sheep and it dodged expertly away. After several attempts her energy was sapped and she was breathing heavily. She tried her inhaler but it was useless; she knew she would certainly fail in her quest now.

Quit.

Search 'Hermes_Walkthrough.doc'
Open C:/documents/Hermes_Walkthrough.doc
Exit
Run 'Herms'
Error
Run 'Hermes'

You are in the Canadian Wilderness. There are Rocky Mountains on all sides. You are carrying a Leather Satchel containing an asthma pump. Your name is Veronica and you are on a quest but as yet have no knowledge of what this might involve.

NORTH

You are in the Canadian Wilderness. There are Rocky Mountains on all sides.

NORTH

You are in the Canadian Wilderness. There are Rocky Mountains on all sides. Dusk is fast approaching. There is a Broken Trail to the West.

WEST

You are on the Broken Trail. You see a creature in the distance. It approaches. It is a Bighorn Sheep. It appears to be lost. Your life is at 90%.

USE PUMP

You use the remainder of your asthma pump to restore health. Your life is at 100%.

KILL SHEEP

You have nothing to kill it with.

WEST

You continue West with a Sheep. You follow the Trail, which turns northwards.

NORTH

You continue North with a Sheep. You fall to the ground and sprain your ankle. Your life is at 50%. You see a strange looking Shaft half-buried in the earth.

TAKE SHAFT

You grip the Shaft.

TAKE SHAFT

You already have a grip on it.

TAKE SHAFT FROM EARTH

You pull the Shaft from the ground revealing a Hunting Knife with a bone handle.

LOOK KNIFE

It is a Hunting Knife with a handle made of bone. It makes a strange rattling noise when you move it.

TAKE KNIFE

You take the Knife and put it in your Satchel.

KILL SHEEP

The Sheep is too far North for you to reach it.

NORTH

You limp North along the Trail, stumble and fracture your knee on a Lump of Rock. Your life is at 20%. You sit on the ground as you are unable to walk. There is a Sheep in the distance.

KILL SHEEP WITH KNIFE

The Sheep is too far away.

CALL TO SHEEP

The Sheep comes back to you.

KILL SHEEP WITH KNIFE

You swipe the Knife towards the Sheep, draining more of your energy. The sound from the Knife causes the Sheep to dodge away. Your life is at 10%.

USE PUMP

Your Asthma Pump is empty.

LOOK ROCK

It is a smooth medium sized Lump of Rock that could be used as a weapon.

KILL SHEEP WITH ROCK.

You pick up the Lump of Rock. It breaks into pieces when you kill the Sheep. Your life is at 5%.

LOOK

You are on a Broken Trail in the Canadian Wilderness. There are Rocky Mountains on all sides. It is dusk. There are pieces of Rock and the carcass of a Bighorn Sheep here.

TAKE ROCK

There is no need to do that.

OPEN SHEEP WITH KNIFE

You use the Knife to gut the Sheep. Inside the carcass you discover a Map, a Compass, a Torch and a Vial of Health. Your life is at 2%.

USE VIAL

You drink the contents of the Vial, restoring your health to 100%.

LOOK MAP

By using the Map and Compass you are able to work out your approximate position. The Map also shows a location marked 'Hermes'. It is night time.

NORTH

It is too dark to go anywhere.

USE TORH

I don't understand that command.

USE TORCH

You turn on the Torch. It emits a faint but sufficient glow.

NORTH

You travel North along the Broken Trail.

USE MAP

You travel through the night using the Map as a guide until you reach a sad-looking Barn in which you shelter. There is a Silver Key on a hook here.

TAKE KEY

There is no room left in your Satchel.

INVENTORY

You are carrying a Leather Satchel, a Knife, a Torch, a Map, a Compass, an empty Vial and an empty Asthma Pump. Your life is at 90%. Your Score is 4/100.

DROP VIAL

You drop the Vial.

TAKE KEY
You take the Key.
LOOK KEY
It is a Silver Key with the word 'Hermes' engraved on it.
QUIT
Do you wish to save your game? Y/N
Y
Your progress has been SAVED.
QUIT
...

WHATEVER HAPPENED TO...?
By Glynne Covell

Dripping on toast
Winkles for tea
Sing something simple
Black and white TV

Doors left on the latch
Sugar on bread
Hopscotch and conkers
Roofs finished with lead

Jack Frost on the windows
Jubblies, gob stoppers
Smogs called 'pea-soupers'
And respect for the coppers

Standing for the anthem
At the end of the flicks
Pathe news and farthings
Lollipops on sticks

Blue bags in white washing
And the use of a mangle
Black and white minstrels
Five Boys chocolate and spangles

Conductors on buses
Steam trains the norm
Planes with propellers
And summers so warm

Iodine on knees
Syrup of figs before bed

Tucked in with warm milk
Together with Ted

Beano and Dandy
Penny for the guy
The old rag and bone man
And books of 'I Spy'

Coal fires and coalmen
With sacks on their heads
Gas lamps and trams
Real blankets on beds

Ink wells and blots
Italic writing and lines
Fear of the teacher
Penny book fines

Now such a mystery
To the young of today
With their androids and tablets
And games that they play

But one day when they're older
No doubt they will say
Whatever happened to those things
That we knew in our day!

JOE RENEWS AN OLD FRIENDSHIP
By Tony Ormerod

It had been a long, tiring and, for Joe Hardy, a frustrating and unproductive day.

When the young idiot, a Yank who had the gall to call himself a Director, finally called a halt to the day's proceedings Joe was not alone in thinking that he was taking part in a real turkey; a stinker that would not even make it onto the Children's Television schedules, never mind selling overseas. So much for the deft British touch usually associated with costume drama.

Thus far he had kept his opinions to himself, even when the rather attractive girl with the cute bonnet and the even cuter face had struck up a conversation with him during the lunch break. Lunch? That was a joke! The BBC must be in more of a financial mess than he had thought. Gone were the two-hour leisurely, boozy affairs he used to relish in the 'old days'. That was, of course, when he was a big name in feature films, before the cute one was born and when the clot of a Director was probably in nappies. He removed his top hat which was another thing that he detested before handing it to a nearby cameraman. "Regency" just did not suit him.

'Well Joe, how's it going then?' He was so deeply immersed in his own thoughts that he had not even noticed someone sidle up to him. It was the clot.

'Oh, hello erm… erm…' he had forgotten the fool's name.

'May I just say Joe,' an arm went around the veteran's shoulder, 'what a great privilege it is for me to direct someone of your stature?'

Taken aback by this glowing tribute, Joe was temporarily lost for words. Was this chap taking the Michael or could he really be serious? Then the consummate actor took over as he found his voice.

'That's very nice of you old son, didn't think you'd know me really.' Modesty did not come naturally to him, but he did his best to fake it.

'Of course, I do. How could anyone forget you? I never dared dream that I, Vince Jones would one day work with the great Joe Hardy!'

So that was his name? Vince Jones; *never heard of him, but never mind* thought Joe as he found himself thawing a little towards "the clot". At least the lad recognised genius when he stumbled onto it. The Director grasped the older man's arm.

'Some of us are going on to the Nag's Head across the road for drinks,' he gushed. 'I'd consider it an honour if you would let me buy you a beer.'

Joe, as always, needed no second invitation.

'That's very decent of you old boy, I'll let you!'

'Great, see you in a few minutes then?'

Looking around the set the veteran actor was disappointed to note that the cute one was no longer around. There was a time, he thought, when girls such as she would have been queuing for his autograph. With a sigh, he unwound and discarded the cravat which, like his topper, was not the sort of thing he felt comfortable in. Then, searching for and eventually finding his overcoat he mooched around the gigantic set until most people had gone. How long had it been since he last used the Nag's Head? Not since his RADA days certainly. The place to be seen 40 years ago, but which for him brought back unpleasant memories, successfully and conveniently pushed to the back of his mind.

He left the studio and made his way across the busy main road before carefully threading his way through a noisy gang of smokers who were braving the night air but blocking the entrance into the pub. The place had changed. Gone were the comfortable armchairs and, at first glance, there appeared to be no sign of furniture; but then, he could see very little beyond the scrum. Looking up he noted the white pristine ceiling which in his time was a disgusting mix of brown and dirty yellow. Like himself, that was a thing of the past, but he was loath to admit it.

Peering around and even standing on tiptoe a little he could not find what he was looking for. There was no sign of the American and, without the necessary cash, he was in no position to approach a bar which, at least, was more or less of the same size and in the same position as he remembered.

Reluctantly, he found himself thinking back over the years. Was it forty years since he last saw her? He had paid dearly for what he had done, with money he could ill afford. Any regrets or shame he may have felt at the time over the way he had treated the girl had been supplanted by relief and the knowledge that he had gotten away with it. After all, Joe had always looked after number one. The din of many voices had subsided, to be replaced by a few murmurings above which Joe distinctly heard one female enquiring whether or not it was 'what's his name? That old actor bloke, you know!' who had walked through the door? Recognition of a sort, which cheered him a little.

Then he heard the laugh. It came from the bar area somewhere on the far side. A happy, carefree sound, something that rolled back the years, but which seemed unbelievable and yet, there could be no mistake. Surely, no one else ever laughed like Jane? There it was again. Elbowing his way through the crowd, excusing himself but nevertheless treading on toes, he reached the bar and saw her; perched on a bar stool, facing him, sipping a tall cocktail through a straw. She had aged somewhat but it was definitely her. Blonde, still attractive, surrounded by people, some of whom he recognised as his fellow actors.

Suddenly, only a few yards from her, Joe realised that he had gotten himself into a situation without giving any thought as to what his reception might be, but before he had time to change his mind, she looked up from her drink and fixed him with a smile.

'Hello Joe, surprised to see me?' She was so matter-of-fact that for a moment or two he found himself speechless.

'Really Joe,' there was that laugh again, 'anyone would think you'd seen a ghost.'

'Jane, Jane.'

'That's my name'. The smile had disappeared.

'Let's talk.' He held her arm and gently helped her off the stool. 'I've not seen you for oh, it must be, let's see…'

'Forty years, Joe,' she interrupted and at the same time removed his hand from around her waist.

'Give us a couple of minutes, won't you?' Joe addressed the people nearest to Jane in a tone that was more a command than a request, but which persuaded them to grudgingly move away to a position further down the bar. Still in sight but out of earshot. At that moment, a couple

158

sitting nearby vacated one of the few tables which allowed him to steer her towards it and then, just in time, stake their claim before others could. Taking a seat, somewhat unsteadily, Joe noted, still clutching her drink but consigning an expensive handbag clumsily out of sight under the table, she fixed him with a stare which frankly disturbed him. He broke the silence.

'What a coincidence Jane.'

'Not quite Joe.' Puzzled, he ploughed on.

'All these years eh, I've often thought about you' he lied, 'all the good times we had, all those parties…'

'Who do you think you're kidding? You might have had a good time but don't include me. Let's face it, you took advantage of me and I was pregnant at 18.'

'Yes, but I helped you, didn't I?' He looked around desperately. Where was the promised drink which he certainly needed now? Out of the corner of his eye, he saw what he was looking for. Holding a drink in each hand the idiot Director had appeared and he was laughing and joking with other members of the cast, almost within touching distance. Jane was in full flow. 'You thought that a lousy four hundred pounds would buy me off, did you?' She removed the straw from her glass and flung it aside before taking a large swig from the contents.'

'Well, it was what you wanted, wasn't it? I mean you did want the, the er…'

'Can't say it, Joe? Abortion, was that the word you were searching for?'

'Well yes, but you disappeared, you simply vanished into thin air. I asked everywhere but…' The old ham spread his arms dramatically and almost knocked a drink out of the hand of the American who had, at last, come to his rescue.

'Hey, you two, glad to see you're getting along!' He stood there looking down at them grinning and clutching the drinks to his chest.

Jane ignored him but, warming to her task, she pointed an accusing finger at Joe.

'If you must know I cleared off to Canada, but don't worry, I did well for myself. In fact, I married an American millionaire.' Glancing ostentatiously at the rather vulgar display of jewellery which adorned her fingers she added. 'I'm the richest widow you'll ever meet.'

Joe, uncomfortable now, looked nervously from one to the other, considering whether or not to continue a conversation that seemingly was no longer held in private.

'Should we be talking like this in front of…?' but it was his turn to be ignored.

'Yes Joe, I suppose I should thank you really. Without you, you swine, I might have married just anybody, someone like you perhaps?'

No chance thought Joe who was stung by her remarks and increasingly embarrassed that their dirty washing was being aired in front of a stranger. He looked up and sure enough, the Yank was still there, hovering, unfazed, still wearing his ridiculous grin and holding on to the drinks.

Jane was not finished. She threw back her head and swallowed the rest of her cocktail then, leaning forward towards Joe, lowering her voice a little, she spoke again.

'Your four hundred pounds, it came in handy. It changed my life.'

'When you had the erm, abortion?'

'I didn't.'

'You didn't what?'

'Have an abortion Joe.'

'But, but, my money, why? What did you…?'

She held up an imperious hand.

'You forget, I was a Catholic, I still am I suppose. Or am I lapsed?' She was slurring her words and looking as though she would burst into tears at any moment.

'Of course, dear,' he reached for her hand, which she smartly withdrew, 'how could I forget?'

He had never known to begin with, and anyway, so what?

She took a deep breath before continuing.

'Your money paid for my airfare to Canada. I couldn't face my parents, but my older sister took me in over there and I had the baby.' She paused and glanced down again at the rings on her fingers, which seemed to cheer her. 'We ended up in the States and landed on our feet.'

Joe had lost interest. She was droning on and the irritating, nosey Director was still standing over them inexplicably unfazed by the turn of events, still holding two drinks. He should mind his own business.

'Is one of those mine matey?' Joe enquired. 'I've been waiting for ages.'

'This is yours, Joe.' He was still smiling.

'What is it?'

'A large brandy.'

'I don't like brandy, you cretin.' At last the grin disappeared.

'I think you might need it'. Jane chipped in. 'Don't you think so Vince?'

Lifting her drink, she was about to add something else, but Vince had other ideas.

'Here's to you Mom and especially to you Joe. Or should I call you "Pop"?

Jane laughed her laugh and sipped her drink. Joe almost choked on his.

FATBERG
By Jan Brown

The smell woke Tomaz. A rotten cabbage stink, powerful, stinging his eyes, like a million overflowing recycling bins. He could hear voices drifting past him, conversations, arguments, and the steady buzz of traffic.

'Help!' He shouted hopefully into brief unexpected silence, thick and heavy, but the moment quickly passed and traffic surged on excitedly towards the next set of lights.

Why was it so dark?

Tomas closed his eyes, trying to ignore the nausea swirling in his stomach.

When he awoke again he felt a little better. His hangover was bearable, although he felt incredibly thirsty, but he was not home cuddled up to Stacey.

Where was he? No, not prepared to admit that he knew where he was, not yet. Then it would be true, real.

Voices.

'I've told Simon to sort himself out or we're finished, I've had enough, Vicky, I really have.'

'Well, I admire you, Carol, you know that.'

Tomaz looked around in the gloom then shouted, 'Hello? Is anyone there?'

'Vicky, did you hear that?'

'What's that, Carol? You hearing voices again, love? Have you got a spare ciggie? I'm right out...'

High heels tapped away into the distance, sounding out their unmistakable click-click, which he had always found very sexy.

Silence.

Feeling his hands and wrists sinking into liquid sludge, Tomaz groaned and tried to haul himself to a standing position. He shrieked and staggered against the sewers' damp, mouldy wall, his dripping hands hanging uselessly before him.

He barely flinched at the sudden blast of an angry lorry horn; he knew that its monstrous wheels couldn't hurt him, not down here, in the sewer. He rinsed what he could off his hands in a trickling gutter and steadied himself against the rough wall.

How did I get down here? Am I really here? Am I dreaming or in a ruddy coma, courtesy of Nigel's California Sunshine?

Tomaz sucked distractedly at his thumb, seeking comfort, ignoring the tainted flavour. He thought of his mum, tiny with the biggest smile, stoutly defending her little boy's right to thumb-suck against the more rigid parenting favoured by his father.

'Help! Help me! I'm down here, please help me!'

Nothing. No one to hear him.

Had he been a poetic man, Tomaz might have thought of his desperate cries being stifled as he was whisked down darkened tunnels into a relentless abyss. He didn't think of these things though as his stomach was still a little tender and poetry had never been a favourite subject.

Turning another corner, it became a little easier to navigate as suffocating darkness evolved into a sort of shadow-land ambience, inviting hope but demanding caution.

'Right!' He ground his teeth together. 'There has got to be a way out of here.'

He resolutely pressed on towards a faint murmuring he had become aware of — a solitary worker, maybe?

'Hey, who's down here?'

Immediately, the sound stopped, and he hesitated, breathing heavily against the sudden silence.

'I know someone's there!'

Hearing the tiniest whimpering response, he dropped to his knees.

My god, is it a dog? Someone's thrown a dog down here.

'Come on boy, here.'

He began crawling through the slime, whistling and patting his trouser legs, adding more layers of muck. When it reared up out of the sewage, Tomaz fell backwards into an overflowing gulley and, like an upended turtle, thrashed about trying to right himself.

He looked up from his watery hollow.

'What the hell are you?'

163

Huge and pallid, with a shapeless liquidity, it definitely wasn't a dog. Tomaz wrinkled his nose at the stench.

The thing looming over him didn't seem to have any eyes, but Tomaz felt it had awareness — after all, it had lurched at him.

He leaned forward, fascinated as its pale, glistening form oozed towards him; its fat, shiny globules dribbling down into the gutter.

'Wow, a fatburger.'

Tomaz had half decided. Yes, he had overindulged on the happy juice, and it was best to just go with the situation.

'No, everyone makes that mistake. Fatburger is an American burger company. I'm a fatberg.'

'I'm not going mad, I'm not going mad, I'm not...am I?'

He looked around warily, suddenly questioning his words. Did he want an answer or not? What was worse? Having a conversation with a fatberg or imagining you were having a conversation with a fatberg?

'You're not real,' he shouted daringly in the general direction of the lumpy mass.

'I disagree. There are lots of us. We're in all the papers. In fact, a lot of paper ends up down here, so there's always something to read and snack on. I've been called a monstrous mass of grease, fat and garbage, if you can believe that.'

It shook itself, seemingly indignant, and Tomaz dodged an onslaught of shimmering fat balls.

'Oooh, I'm sweating badly. Must be quite warm today.'

'Noooo. Tomaz slapped vigorously at his own head. 'This is not happening. It's not right.'

'Easy duck. What's up with you?'

'I need to get out.' He could hear his heart thumping. 'I'm stuck down here, and I'm talking to a load of stinking, congealed lard.'

'Well there's no need to insult me.'

Bits of it seemed to form into lips and pucker up like a disapproving mother-in-law.

'I don't know what you're up to do I? Anyway, I'm off to look for a cosy drain to block...bungalows I love, or conversions.'

It chattered on, becoming muffled and difficult to isolate from the general buzz of traffic above ground.

Tomaz remained leaning against the coarse, curved wall for what felt like a long time, endeavouring to slow his breathing, trying to think and yet, not think too much.

'I blame you for this, Nigel.' he muttered as he trudged on. 'You can stuff any idea of me being your best man now.'

He moved cautiously now, stopping every few yards to listen, look up and around, and hope. He knew he had travelled, although he had lost all grasp of time or location.

He almost missed the tiny spark of light above him.

'Hey!' He screamed. 'Help me get out of here. Look down!'

A few muttering voices grew in volume and number as interest spread. Tomaz swallowed, trying to inspire his raw throat.

'Help me. I'm down here. Please, look down.'

Finally, bemused but willing hands wrenched away the grating and hauled him up to freedom. He blinked away the shock of natural light and noise, grinning at his rescuers as they enquired if he needed anything.

Tomaz thought for a moment.

'Yeh, has anyone got a fag?'

'Blimey mate, you stink, probably get yourself sorted with a bath first.' The yellow-jacketed workman chuckled, and the regular beat of London life moved on.

THE VISIT
By Julia Gale

You could have knocked me down with a feather when I received the letter to say that our housing association estate was to compete against others locally in the annual 'Best Kept Estate' Competition.

I took the letter to the housing office's committee, of which I am the chairperson. They all agreed that I was the right person to organise this, and it would be a big morale boost for the other residents if we won. This was going to be a tough assignment, I knew that, but what I had not bargained for was the massive surprise that lay in store for me.

The first task was to persuade someone to come and open the summer fete that was to coincide with the judging. Nobody seemed to be interested except for Sir Robert Bentley, a local dignitary, but even he told us that he could not come as he had "other engagements" on that day but would be delighted to send his daughter Caroline to do the job as it happened to be her 20th birthday and she had "nothing else to do." Caroline Bentley had a reputation for being an obnoxious young woman. However, we did not want to appear ungrateful to Sir Robert and accepted his kind offer.

I had to organise a team to scrub off graffiti and make sure everybody had their houses in clean and tidy condition in case they received a visit from Caroline or one of the judges.

This was not an easy task. You should have heard some of the verbal abuse I got, especially from old Mr Thomas down the road. Odd sort; he likes to keep himself to himself. He told me, "I want nothing to do with that toffee-nosed little upstart; she won't be welcome in my house," and that was putting it politely - not surprising though when you see the state he lives in. Mr Thomas was not the only one who opposed the idea - most of the estate did as well.

However, there were a few willing volunteers, some friends of mine, and my boys; we soon knuckled down to tidying the place up. It took longer than we first thought - thank God we were given six months to do it.

I had not quite realised the state of disrepair. Broken windows had to be replaced, chewing gum and other things removed from the pavements, graffiti removed and the playground restored so that children could play safely again. The list seemed unending, and I was glad the council paid for it all. Eventually, the builders came and started on our smart new community centre; it took ages to build and it was still not quite ready on opening day. Not surprising really, when you think of all the tea and ultra-long lunch breaks they had taken. Still, after months of hard work, we got the place spick and span two weeks before Caroline Bentley's arrival.

For a long time, I worked as a cleaner on the Bentley Estate. They have a grand manor house in the country. Sir Robert Bentley inherited his knighthood from his great grandfather, who made his money through baking biscuits or something.

I got on well with Sir Robert's first wife Sylvia, a very frail woman, who could not have children of her own. Sir Robert is not a nice man and it was common knowledge that he had an eye for the ladies. He blamed Sylvia for not being able to bear him children; why she stayed with him I cannot tell. However, she was very good to me, even helped me out with the cleaning, and showed great interest in my children - I had four at the time.

Sylvia died and Sir Robert soon got himself a new wife who sacked everyone who displeased her; me included. I was carrying twins at the time. That was just over 20 years ago. I had to give up the girl twin for adoption but that is another story. Some years later, I found out that Sir Robert's second wife had given birth to a son who would inherit his father's title.

The big day had finally arrived and there was great excitement in the air. Suddenly, everybody wanted to help with the final preparations. It is strange how people suddenly want to know you and help after the hard graft has finished.

It seemed as though the whole estate had come out to line the streets with eager anticipation (or just plain curiosity) to await Caroline's arrival. She arrived thirty minutes late in a huge white chauffeur-driven limo; eventually she stepped out of the car. She looked nothing like I imagined. She was tiny, only 5 feet 3 inches, with long ginger hair neatly tied back; she looked frail, and petite and completely overwhelmed by the attention she was getting from the local press.

She was, in my opinion, very inappropriately dressed for an occasion like this and looked very uncomfortable. She wore a white flowing ball-gown type dress with gold-coloured sequins (I'm sure I have seen a dress similar to that in Primark for a fiver) and on her feet she had a pair of gold-coloured diamante high-heeled sandals. Pale faced and with tears beginning to form in her eyes, Caroline stood on the spot, terrified by the attention she was getting. She looked about twelve years old.

I eventually managed to persuade my youngest son Peter, after he had stopped staring and drooling at her, to lead her down to the community centre. Gently, he wrapped his jacket around her and held her hand. It was at that moment I realised there was something familiar about her.

I would like to have said that the ceremony went without a hitch but it did not. As soon as Caroline cut the ribbon with the ridiculously oversized scissors, she stumbled and fell, breaking one of her expensive shoes, ripping her dress and twisting her ankle in the process. She was in such a sorry state that Peter immediately went to her aid and, with some of his friends, escorted her, limping, back to our house.

At home I made Caroline a cup of sweet tea and ran her a bath as I could see she was still in shock from her accident. When she finally emerged from the bathroom, I lent her a pair of jeans and an old baggy jumper of mine, as by chance we appeared to be the same size. She went on to tell me that her stepmother had told her only that morning about her adoption as a baby. She then said her stepmother had also told her that her real mother used to be an employee of her father's and, at that time, had lived on our estate. She was determined to find out whether her mother still lived here, but as her stepmother had not given Caroline her real mother's name she did not know where to start. Could I help her?

Of course I can, when I am certain that she is mine.

When she had had fully recovered from her earlier ordeal and I was fully certain that she was ok, my son Peter (who had left the room whilst we were talking), suggested that he take her for a drive to show her around and perhaps go for a drink - it was both their birthdays after all. Caroline agreed and left with him. I hope they do not get too close. How do I tell them they could be brother and sister?

In the meantime, I will just go back to what I am good at - cleaning up other people's messes.

STATEMENT
By Richie Stress

The lady down the road, she starved to death,
she smoked away adipose in her skin.
They say the walls are dog shit brown.
They found a solitary sachet of salad cream
and even that was past its sell by date.

Now there has to be an inquiry -
to find out why. She wasn't on anybody's lists;
she never wanted to be - I could tell.
One glance from her wrinkled walnut face as
she tight-roped home – balancing boxes of Bensons:

'They've raised the tax again', blurting like a vomit,
'this bloody government will be the death of me.'

The stupid biddy never made a will,
I reckon house is worth a few quid, mind.

THE WRONG SUITCASE
By Tony Ormerod

My baggage had been packed with loving care prior to leaving my rundown hotel, and there were no problems when I passed through the ramshackle airport on my departure. However, I knew that any London airport would be a different matter.

'I picked up the wrong suitcase.'

The policeman gripped my arm even tighter and gave the kind of shrug that suggested he'd heard it before. 'Kindly come this way, sir, we don't want any fuss, sir, do we?'

He was built like a brick privy so it was unlikely that I would be making any fuss at all as I was marched beyond the red and green customs zones. At least his dog had stopped barking.

'I tell you, this case is not mine,' I was pleading with him. 'It looks like mine, it's the same colour, and the same size, but it's not mine. I've made a mistake.' Privately, I thought it did seem slightly heavier than I remembered.

'You certainly have, sir, trying to put one over on my pal Rex here.' The officer glanced down affectionately at the German Shepherd, which was now furiously wagging its tail, obviously pleased that a drug trafficker had been apprehended and still dutifully sniffing away at the suitcase and my private parts every few seconds. I don't like dogs at the best of times.

I took another look at the case, but it was missing the luggage label which would at least have identified the real owner. I anticipated the worst as I was manoeuvred into a small room where, seated behind a table, another stern-faced giant of a man in plain clothes was waiting.

'Well done, Dawson.' He rose to his feet and turned to address me.

'Passport?' he demanded curtly. No "sir" from him, I noticed. When my arm was reluctantly released, I fished into the inside pocket of my jacket and produced the familiar maroon booklet; at the same time, the suitcase was swiftly transferred from my grasp and onto the table. There followed a brief examination of my passport.

'What have we got here then Mr. Ormondroid?' I winced at the

171

mangling of my name but decided against correcting him.

'I keep telling your chum here that this is not my case, and I haven't got a clue as to what's inside it.'

'Keys please.' A large hand stretched out towards me.

'Have you been listening to me, it's not my...'

'Oh, rightio, it's not yours, so we'll just have to rely on brute force, then won't we?' He sat down, reached under the table and produced an industrial sized pair of bolt cutters which, within seconds, had sliced through the formidable padlock. Rather theatrically, he flung open the lid. For a moment or two he glanced down and, puzzled, he took out a small package that he proceeded to rip open. Rex, whose tail had not stopped wagging, leapt from his standing to attention position and onto the table. Without pausing he snatched the item from the chief interrogator's hand and succeeded in knocking him backwards onto the floor, chair still sticking obstinately to a generous backside. In spite of my bias against dogs, I found myself warming to Rex.

'What the hell, Dawson, this case is full of dog food. Tins and packets!' His subordinate hurried forward to restrain the Alsatian, which was tucking into something. Meanwhile the embarrassed officer was trying to assist his boss, who was heavily engaged in attempting to regain his feet and his composure. Meanwhile I leant forward and saw for myself that the suitcase was chock full of doggy delights. I could not help laughing.

'Think it's funny, Omeroid, do you?' The boss was red faced and not amused.

'Oh yes, very. And it's *Ormerod*, O-r-m, oh never mind.'

'Bonios sir, this is a packet of Bonios.' Dawson indicated an empty half-eaten wrapping. 'They're his favourite, sir.' Rex barked once as if in confirmation.

I snatched my passport from the table, thanked them for the entertainment, and took my leave, pausing only to remind them again that it was not my suitcase. Somewhere, in or around Gatwick airport, someone who took pet ownership to new heights was in possession of my drugs.

THE WINTER SEA
By Richard Miller

It was 2 January, the morning was cold and overcast, and I had just left my house in Swanage town centre. I needed to go for a long walk to clear away the cobwebs and have some exercise after two days of drinking and partying. I headed to the beach, which was only a few minutes' walk away. The plan was to walk along the beach as far as possible before heading inland and taking a path to Old Harry's Rocks. From there, I would move on to the Bankes Arm pub in Studland Bay: a wonderful pub with a fine view of the bay.

Ambling along the beach, I stopped every so often to skim stones over the water. It was freezing cold and the air felt damp. The water was choppy and grey and some of the waves were high; strong winds coming in from the English Channel nearly blew me off my feet on a number of occasions.

Very few people were out – only the brave, and most of them were dog walkers. As it was cold I suspected that many of the locals and visitors were still sleeping off the excesses of alcohol or else consuming vast quantities of coffee. I reckoned that several people were making vows that they would never drink again but, knowing the good folk of Swanage, those promises wouldn't last long. Looking out over Swanage Bay I could see the Isle of Wight shrouded in a mist. A few boats were dancing around in the water and a ferry was heading from Poole towards France.

Coming to the point of the beach where I would have to head inland, I took one last look at Swanage Bay and noticed something moving in the water, about a hundred yards from the beach. I first thought it was a buoy, but it was the wrong shape. Taking the binoculars from my rucksack, I gazed out at the water. Whatever was bobbing in the water – and I still couldn't work out what it was – appeared to be heading towards the beach. It didn't look like a swimmer. The more I looked, the closer the object came towards the beach and I still couldn't make out what it was. Perhaps it was a mine left over from World War Two and I should contact the Coast Guard:

mines were often found floating off the South Coast. It was then that I was able to work out what the object was: it was a human - but not a swimmer or diver.

Being a keen amateur military historian I recognised that the person who had emerged from the sea was wearing the uniform of a U.S. Ranger from World War Two. I thought the drink was playing tricks with my mind and I was seeing things. It wouldn't have been the first time.

The U.S. Rangers considered themselves to be the equivalent of Britain's Commandos. I had not read of any re-enactment events and surely this was the wrong time of the year. Even if there was a re-enactment, wouldn't a boat have picked up someone who had fallen overboard?

The Ranger, who was partially covered in seaweed, saw me and headed towards me. "Where am I?" he asked, in what sounded like an accent from the Southern States of the USA.

Still recovering from the shock, I said with a faltering voice: "You're in Swanage Bay."

Looking baffled, he uttered: "I was in Swanage a couple of weeks ago and it certainly didn't look like this!" He pointed to the beach huts. "And what are you wearing? I don't often see you Brits wearing jeans and leather jacket." He noticed one of the badges I was wearing and exclaimed: "Who or what are the Rolling Stones?"

I pondered: even someone who doesn't listen to music must have heard of the Rolling Stones. A dark thought crossed my mind, one so bizarre that I tried to dismiss it. Perhaps he was a ghost, or, more strangely, a time-traveller from WW2. Had I watched too many episodes of Doctor Who?

"My name is Richard," I said. "I often wear jeans and a leather jacket, and you must have heard of the Rolling Stones: the rock and roll band who also play the blues. They are big in the States."

"I've heard of blues but not rock and roll. What the hell is that? They must be big in a different part of the States from me."

A million thoughts rushed through my mind and I had many questions. I wasn't sure which one to ask first.

"I notice that you're wearing a U.S. Rangers uniform from World War Two. Do you mind if I ask which unit?"

"No, you may not." A Mercedes car drove past. The Ranger stared at the car and then at me. "I ain't seen an automobile like that before but I recognise the badge and I can't believe that people in this country would drive a car made by your enemy. And talking of automobiles, where are the military vehicles? There were loads two weeks ago!"

I knew that I had a lot of explaining to do. "Look, I'm not a spy; I like military history." The Ranger, looking confused, raised an eyebrow. "I wouldn't be surprised if you don't believe me, but the year is 2015 and WW2 finished nearly seventy years ago. The Allies were victorious."

Being told that the year was 2015 must have troubled him as much it did me about seeing someone who was apparently from WW2. Or perhaps he was a very good actor out trying to trick the locals.

"You're right, I don't believe you. Just take me to someone in my or your army, or just the police. I'm cold and wet and not in the mood to be mucked about by someone who thinks I'm from history."

"Let's find a newsagent," I said. "I'll buy a paper which will show the date."

As we headed down the high street we were passed by several people, a few of whom recognised me. "Who's your friend, Richard? Has he been at a fancy dress party?"

I looked at the Ranger and sensed that he was becoming more and more angry. "Ignore those people, they've had too much to drink." It sounded pathetic but I couldn't think of anything better to say.

Arriving at the newsagent, I went in and bought a copy of the Daily Telegraph. I handed over the paper to the Ranger, making a point to show him the date.

"So it's January 2, 2015. £1.50 for a newspaper, that's a lot of money - and what happened to pounds, shillings and pence?"

"Look, you said that you're cold and wet. You can go to my place and put on some dry clothes. You look about the same size as me. It would also be a better place to chat. I only live a few minutes from here. You can also ring the U.S. Embassy and the police."

He was hesitant but the thought of dry clothes and the opportunity to ring the U.S. Embassy must have swayed him.

Arriving at my house I showed him to a room where he could change and pointed out the bathroom. Leaving him for a few minutes would allow me to compose myself and think about what questions to ask and whether I should phone anyone other than the police and U.S. Embassy: perhaps the Ministry of Defence. After a while the Ranger emerged and asked for a coffee. I offered a whisky as well but he said he didn't drink. Taking the coffee, he sat down and looked around the room, noticing my collection of books, records and whisky bottles. I went over to the bookshelf, pulled out a general history of WW2 and handed it to him along with the recently purchased Daily Telegraph.

Switching between the paper and the book, his expression changed from confusion to intrigue and even a hint of anger. "Look, I don't know who you are or what's going on but I'm going to ask you a lot of questions and I want straight answers. By the way, thanks for the coffee and clothes."

"I'm as confused as you! Hopefully from reading the paper and bits of the book you are beginning to believe that it is actually 2015. If it is, you must believe that whatever you tell me is no longer a secret. I have two questions for you. What's your name and what date do you think it is?"

"My name is Dave and for me the date is 28 April 1944." The date rang a bell in my mind. He continued: "Okay, I'm willing to take a risk and trust you but just remember, no funny business."

Sipping at his coffee Dave took another look at the paper. "So we have a black president in the States. Barack Obama. I wonder what he's like. Roosevelt is a hard act to follow. You say that the war is over? I wonder how Roosevelt celebrated."

I didn't have the heart to tell him that the Roosevelt passed away before the end of the war.

"The last thing I remember was being in a boat approaching Slapton Sands. You know the area?" I nodded. "I was based in Weymouth so used to come along to Swanage on occasions, a nice town. Anyway, as I was saying, I remember being in Lyme Bay and a German E-Boat heading towards my landing craft and firing a torpedo which hit us and I ended up in the water. I was knocked out as I hit the side of the boat. It was a right shambles; there should have been no E-boats in the water. I wonder if it will mean the invasion of France being put back. I guess that's down to Generals Eisenhower and Montgomery to worry about."

"Were you taking part in Operation Tiger?" I asked. Operation Tiger was an exercise carried out in April of 1944 to practise for the

D-Day landings. It had turned to carnage when German E-Boats had attacked and sunk landing craft. Many were left dead and injured.

"So you know the name of the exercise. I guess that means it's no longer a secret."

"As I said, I'm not a spy but I'm just interested in military history. World War Two finished nearly seventy years ago. The invasion of France took place on 6 June 1944 and the Allies were finally victorious the next year."

I continued: "After the invasion it wasn't all plain sailing before the Germans eventually surrendered in May 1945. Their allies, the Japanese, capitulated a few months later. As I said, it wasn't all plain sailing - I can tell you about that later, or you can read about it in my books. With the Americans, British and Canadians advancing from the West and the Soviet Union from the East, it was a matter of time before victory in Europe."

The Ranger was shocked when I told him about the dropping of atomic bombs on two cities in Japan.

The next hour or so was spent with me telling him about how Churchill was defeated in the election of 1945 and re-elected in 1951. The Ranger was surprised that Churchill had been defeated in 1945 and thought that the British people were ungrateful. I explained that people were grateful, but society had changed and people wanted a new leader and government. When Churchill died in 1965, tens of thousands paid their respects. He was visibly upset when I told him that Roosevelt died a month before the war in Europe had ended.

"It would have been lovely for him to have seen the end of the war and join in the celebrations."

Dave was surprised when I told him that Eisenhower served two terms as U.S. President. "I didn't think he would become a politician, but I guess if you've been in charge of one of the largest armies in history you learn a lot about leadership."

He wasn't that surprised about the frosty relationship between the Soviet Union and the West. "There had been signs of that during the war!" he exclaimed. I explained that the relationship had improved but there were still some tense moments. As we discussed the last seventy years I wasn't sure how much I should tell him. Would those at the Embassy want me to tell him what had happened?

I was dying to ask him so many questions about what he could remember after he fell from the boat. Had he been trapped in a 'time bubble' and somehow escaped? Was he a ghost? I always thought that ghosts couldn't be felt but I had touched him. He seemed real. Or perhaps he was a con artist who had entered the water from the other side of the headland on the northern side of Swanage Bay? But he seemed genuinely shocked and surprised when I told him about Roosevelt and Eisenhower. Perhaps I should give him a piece of wrong information and see how he reacted.

"There are several more questions you may wish to ask me, but it would be best if you spoke to someone in your Embassy as I'm not an American," I said.

Dave accepted that. We sat silently for a moment and then out of the blue I mentioned the first moon landing in August 1970. I knew that the first moon landing had taken place in July 1969 and had deliberately given the wrong date. The Ranger seemed genuinely surprised: "That's a big step from the transport planes I flew!" Then suddenly: "I'd like to speak to the U.S. Embassy now. Can you phone them for me?"

He looked with bemusement at the phone with no cables as I made the call. Passing the phone to him, I would have loved to hear what the person in the Embassy was saying. After a few minutes, Dave handed the phone back to me. "They'll be sending someone along but want to know your address."

After giving my address I hung up. "Were you married - or should that be are you married?"

"Yes, and to a local lass. We were expecting our first child in July of 1944."

He gave her first and married and maiden names. The married name was unusual. "No. I can't believe it. If it's the same person as I think it is, she is my grandmother and she is still alive."

"No!" The Ranger who could be my long lost grandfather looked surprised. I knew he had been American but that was all. Gran was very reluctant to talk about him. All she had ever said was that he had been killed in action and there were no photographs of him.

Still in a state of shock I picked up my phone and dialled my grandmother. "Gran, how's things? I'll be up later to see you. I've someone with me. He knows you and I have to say I'm pleased to meet him."

"That's nice," my gran said, sounding bemused.

"I'll hand the phone to him."

Dave took a deep breath. Fighting back the tears, he said: "Hi Grace, it's Dave. Long time, no see."

I left the room. It was time to leave them alone for a while. We would all meet up later for what could be the most bizarre reunion ever.

FIRST TIME ABROAD
By Glynne Covell

I was extremely nervous. All this talk about going to South Africa scared me, quite frankly, and I was certainly not looking forward to September when we were to leave.

'It's such a long way to fly,' I complained to my brother.

'Look, I'm going to be with you all the way,' he reassured me. 'Remember that you have flown before, just not abroad and obviously not so far. Once you're up there, it doesn't matter about the distance. Do you remember Dad telling us that when confronted with something we feel we do not have the courage to do, we must have faith? Be strong, be determined and also think beyond the challenge. How proud you will feel when you have achieved this. Let's think about being there too. That glorious warmth!'

My brother had always inspired confidence in me. Even when I had made my first flight, he had encouraged me to be strong then. I had always followed him, looked up to him, being myself always the careful, cautious, nervous one. But this time, I had to be brave. I had to go. There was no choice. The dog days of summer were with us. Late August and settled weather had passed by all too quickly and the day of reckoning was upon us.

We were leaving early the following morning and I slept little that night. Instead, I lay watching the moon as it slowly rose then, later, the sky as it turned pink in the east, the sun gradually nudging over the horizon. It was going to be a fine day to leave England.

Dawn and we were ready for take-off. Assembled together, the noise was incredible as we all stood awaiting the signal for departure. There it was. We had the green light and, one by one, we took flight.

I was exhilarated. Looking down on the place that I had called home for several months, I felt so thankful to have been born in such a glorious setting. I had learned to fly, to look for food and to roost in this wonderful farmland. Now I was able to join the great migration to warmer climes in South Africa for the winter.

I glanced across to my extended family of swallows who had all gathered together in the early hours of the day, ready to travel south. We were as one. It would not be easy. I knew it was a long way over Europe and then across the vast continent of Africa. But this was what we had evolved to do. This was what we were compelled to do in order for our species to survive – and survive I would. I smiled to myself, feeling proud to be part of such a very grand plan.

PENSIVE
By Richie Stress

My nib and ball
points; precisely positioned,
scuttling nimbly over pulp
forming shopping listing prose.

Throwing alphabet shapes,
conducting doodle dances.
I formulate facts onto charts,
inscribing pathways.

Conceived in inkwell and feather
and primed on dictated rumour: -
Invaders! *Button and Touch-Screen*,
TAKE WHAT IS MINE BY RIGHT.
Cutting and pasting the jostled words.

LOOKING FOR MAYA
By Jan Brown

He was the first one to venture back – maybe the only one. Looking for Maya had drawn Tomei back to the old market quarter, now sombre and still. He had a memory of the wooden huts and cracked pavements heaving with the raw brutality of existence. Once they had found a tiny baby abandoned among the rejected vegetation, and of course Maya had wanted to save it but he knew that ultimately you could only save yourself.

He stood cautiously now at the top of the street, breathing shallowly in the stagnant silence, his attention held by moisture glistening on the rooftops. Each individual raindrop twinkled briefly in the morning greyness before releasing itself. Why had he come here? What had he hoped to find? He shuddered, withdrew deep inside his thick woollen jacket and took a few tentative steps further into the village. Her shop was still there, shuttered and boarded, blank and dead but for the stubby unkempt tree somehow emerging from the building itself.

'Maya!' he screamed.

Only the crows responded, clamouring angrily as they unfurled their black cloaks and shrieked until Tomei covered his ears. Slowly their fury abated into dulled, puzzled clicks as they hunched together, seeking comfort. Finally, the few remaining leaves were motionless in the chill air, there was no wind, no relieving breeze; the thick silence was absolute.

Tomei listened intently for long moments before turning away. He wouldn't stay any longer.

'There's nothing here,' he whispered, 'I've lost her.'

Moving away from the shop front Tomei took one last look back before heading towards the cinder path that signalled the route out of the village, his footsteps now crunching and purposeful.

Maya watched his departure from the security of the old bank building, its thick walls thankfully standing strong against recent onslaughts. A folly of bricks and mortar thrown up among the transient shacks and lean-tos, Maya had long ceased to acknowledge that she too had mocked its construction, now she simply gave thanks for its existence. She clutched the baby in her arms, gently soothing her murmurs; she had named her Hope.

ABOUT THE AUTHORS

The TEN GREEN JOTTERS of Sidcup:

Jan Brown
Jan Brown, aka Emily the Writer, has always loved writing, ambitiously penning her own Starsky & Hutch story at the age of 12, although she never actually allowed anyone else to read it.

Jan has had a number of articles, interviews and short stories published and is a prize winner in, and regular contributor to, The Monthly Seagull magazine and to the Charlton Athletic fanzine. She lives with her partner and two cats, Clive and Jorge, who are named after her footballing heroes.

Glynne Covell
Glynne's "Carpe Diem" attitude to life has found her trekking in New Guinea and the foothills of the Himalayas', hot air ballooning and, closer to home, climbing Big Ben and the O2. London born, she is yet descended from the French Huguenots.

Married, with two children, and grandchildren, her hobbies of travelling, history and calligraphy all have links with her writing for which she has a very special passion (this, and chocolate!). She is delighted to be able to contribute to this, the first anthology by the Ten Green Jotters of Sidcup.

Julia Gale
Originally from Carlisle, then brought up in Southampton, Julia moved to London in 1995 after marrying her husband, Colin. Julia was a prodigious early reader as a child. Always with a book in her hand this may well have fuelled her desire to become an author, and she began by writing poems for the local church magazine. Over the years she has had a variety of jobs but since being married has been a full time mother and house wife, occasionally finding time to do

voluntary work; with Colin, she has two grown up daughters and a disabled son. Her hobbies are cooking and gardening.

Her observations on people, the real life situations they find themselves in and life's many ups and downs are reflected in her stories.

C.G Harris

C. G Harris hails from Kent, England, U.K He is the winner of the *William Van Wert Award 2018* for a fiction short story. His book *Light and Dark: 21 Short Stories* was shortlisted for the *"Words for the Wounded" Georgina Hawtrey-Woore Award for Independent Authors* and has received critical acclaim. His second collection of stories is due for release at Easter 2020.

He has a wife, two daughters, two grandchildren, one dog and a cat. He plays the guitar, ukulele and juggles...although not necessarily all at the same time.

A.J.R. Kinchington

A competition win at eleven years old was the start of life-long story telling for A.J.R. Kinchington.

A twenty-five year career in psychotherapy working with clients on 'Stories that Heal' gave little time to write for pleasure.

Retired, but by no means finished, she is currently writing a memoir of her Scottish heritage.

Richard Miller

Richard has lived most of his life in Sidcup, birthplace of the Ten Green Jotters. Although much of his working career was spent in London as a Network and Telecommunications Manager in a Government Department, his job also required him to visit more exotic locations including Barbados. India, South Africa and Thailand. Switching from writing technical documents to penning something more creative has proved challenging but rewarding.

He is a season ticket holder at Chelsea (he has followed the club for more years than he cares to remember) and enjoys real ale, whisky, blues music and history. At home Richard has several hundred books and records plus over forty bottles of single malt whisky. He is a member of a number of historical societies.

Tony Ormerod
Derby born, and dreaming of journalism, at 16 Tony inexplicably rejected a job offer with the local *Evening Telegraph*. Employment in the warm bosom of Local Government beckoned and then, migrating way down South [Hove], he progressed to Bromley Council where he was later declared surplus to requirements. A career in financial services led to early retirement and an ambition to do nothing was achieved.

Occasionally, this idleness is interrupted by articles published in the aforementioned newspaper plus a couple more in the 'Best of British' magazine. After 50 years he remains married to the same lovely wife. She pleads anonymity.

Richie Stress
Richie has always liked words. He has used them to write short stories, scripts for television and award winning poetry. In 2008 he was talked into studying for a Creative Writing degree by a very enthusiastic lady from the Open University…which he completed a mere seven years later. He also presents regular podcasts together with his partner where he is under strict instructions not to be crude or use bad language. He lives with a diabetic cat called Clive.

Dina Sullivan
South London born and bred, the City of London was home for most of Dina's working life of over 30 years in banking. Since then, having (just about) shaken off the preoccupation with number crunching and spreadsheets, she has found her creative side, namely oil painting and, more importantly, fiction writing; she is currently working on her first novel which she hopes to publish in 2020.

Joining the Ten Green Jotters has, by her own admission, been of immense value in developing her fiction writing, enabling her to contribute a single (albeit a rather long) 'short' story to this anthology. Dina hopes you enjoy reading it as much as she enjoyed writing it.

Janet Winson
Janet is delighted to be a contributor of three stories to this anthology, thus fulfilling her long-held ambition to be a writer. This ambition began at an early age; like many a child in London's post war Britain she and her sister found that the local library provided an avenue to both reading pleasure and, in Janet's case, an inspiration for writing her own stories and poems.

Having a natural feel for writing, her love of words has never foundered and has been a prop through times of change and all the busy years of being a mum, combined with a long working life in the NHS.

Now, in her retirement, as one of the Ten Green Jotters her instinct as a writer has been given a new lease of life.

Lightning Source UK Ltd.
Milton Keynes UK
UKHW021134271219
355981UK00014B/1066/P

9 780244 531676